Running South

Running South

Ritchie Allen Greer

Illustrations by Gail Weissman

authorHOUSE®

AuthorHouse™ LLC
1663 Liberty Drive
Bloomington, IN 47403
www.authorhouse.com
Phone: 1-800-839-8640

Published by AuthorHouse   04/29/2014

ISBN: 978-1-4969-0678-6 (sc)
ISBN: 978-1-4969-0677-9 (e)

Library of Congress Control Number: 2014907531

Special thanks to Matthew Eldridge, Gail Weissman, and Malou Tecson.

Chapter 1

My name is Isaac Dawson and the story I'm about to tell you, you won't find in any history book or hear about in any classroom. It had basically remained forgotten, at least up until now . . .

It all started in the sweltering summer of 1864. Although it was so many years ago, I swear to you I can still see the fields just as clear as if I were standing in them today.

As I think back on that time and place, I don't have to remind myself that there was a certain beauty in it: the way the sun hung silently in the bright sky, the way the thousands of cotton plants swayed back and forth in unison, the way the lush green plants emerged and stretched out from the chocolate brown soil which ultimately collided with the ocean blue horizon, and the way the wind sounded as it ruffled through the reeds around you. It was a symphony of well-orchestrated sights and sounds that seemed to be put together for my sole benefit—almost like a gift from God and Mother Nature herself. There's no doubt those moments could take you away, if you let it.

But back in those days, us slaves weren't supposed to waste time daydreaming or appreciating the scenery. That kind of thing would get you into serious trouble. Even so, I would always find a moment to stand tall, close my eyes, and take a big, deep breath. In those moments, I would imagine myself somewhere else. Maybe on a tall mountain. Maybe by a beach, watching the ocean brush against the sand. Maybe even in a classroom somewhere, listening to stories about people and places in history. As pretty as the fields could be, I was always disappointed when I opened my eyes again and found myself standing right where I'd been a minute before.

My only comfort and my only regret was that my family was also there with me in those fields. You see, my family and I had the distinct and prestigious honor of picking cotton for one of the South's most ruthless slave owners. His name was Jefferson Tomstin III, and his family had owned my family for longer than anyone cared to remember. I was born a slave under Tomstin's employment. My brother, sister, my mother, even my father were all born in the ramshackle cabins that we called home. It was all we knew.

Although Master Tomstin was a cold and heartless man, he was no dummy. As the grandson of a slave owner, he was handed down all the tricks of the trade. He knew how to keep the laborers working. He knew how to keep every man, woman, and child productive. He was also very learned on how to keep order in the fields.

So to keep every one of us working at peak efficiency, Master Tomstin had hired on a Slave Master by the name of Cornelius Slate to not only oversee the work being done but to make sure that we all knew our place.

Slate was tall and thin, and had the kind of tough, leathery face hardened by a lifetime of failures and disappointments. To me, he had almost a military way about him. I had seen a few Confederate soldiers on the plantation over the past couple of years and Mr. Slate always reminded me of them. Maybe it was the way he sat straight up in the saddle like he had a beanpole tied around his back. Maybe it was the way his eyes were always searching, like a soldier looking for a threat. Or maybe it was because of the way he looked at us, the slaves, like we were the enemy he was facing, like he hated us more than anything on earth.

I remember thinking that the hatred towards us wasn't towards us at all. I would like to think that the hatred was more within, like there was an unresolved battle going on inside him that had nothing to do with us; a battle that he was desperately trying to hide.

I never dared ask Mr. Slate himself. That would be a right stupid thing to do. I would do my best to even keep from looking at the man. Every slave in those fields was afraid to make even the slightest rule infraction while under his watch. He had a taste for the whip. Pa even said that half the lashes Slate handed out were just because he was bored and wanted something to do. If I'd had any money, I would have bet every penny that Pa was right. Only a plain fool would deliberately go against Master Tomstin *or* Mr. Slate.

As it so happened, that's exactly what I was doing on that fateful summer morning. The sun was just brightening up the sky, cutting through the thin clouds that the night had left behind. The air was still cool and inviting, and the river that Georgeo and I sat next to was quiet and peaceful.

"The rain poured down onto the tin roof," I read aloud, squinting my eyes at the book in my lap. Though I knew the words, they felt strange in my mouth, like I couldn't quite wrap my lips around them properly. I was making great progress, but they still felt foreign on my tongue.

Reading was a tricky thing for a ten-year-old boy who had never done it before. I had learned to speak at an early age—earlier than my siblings, according to my parents—but reading was something different entirely. I knew how the words sounded, but they seemed so different when they were written down. Imagine hearing a sound and then trying to draw how it sounded. That's what words seemed like to me. I could understand and recognize them more and more as time went on, but it was still strange that those black markings on the paper were actually the same words that I was speaking.

I pushed the wire-framed glasses up on the bridge of my nose and focused once more on the page. "The rain poured down onto the tin roof, making music for all to hear."

"That's right!" Georgeo said with a smile. "That's good! Keep going!"

"Each drop was a call to me," I continued, causing Georgeo to nod enthusiastically beside me. "Each drop whispered my name, asking me to come into the storm."

"Fantastic," Georgeo said. "I'm telling you, you've come a long way since we started!"

Every week, he would make a similar statement. I think it genuinely surprised him how fast I caught on. It was probably because for the past several months, these secret classes with him had been the thing I looked forward to most in the world. I would focus all my energy on what I had learned and on what I was *going* to learn.

The reason I was doing this was not only to spend time with Georgeo. There was something else—something bigger, something greater. You see, the truth is, I wanted to be a writer. Not someone who could just write his name, but someone who could use words to weave magic into even the simplest of stories. But to do that, you must first learn to read, which I knew wasn't allowed.

And I wasn't the only one who was risking a lot down by the river. You see, Georgeo was, in fact, Georgeo Tomstin, the son of Master Jefferson Tomstin himself. A slave owner's son befriending one of the slaves, well . . . it was obvious why we had to keep our lessons a secret. If we met more than once a week, we stood a better chance of being found out. If Georgeo was discovered teaching me to read, I knew I would get a beating that would likely leave me useless for weeks, if not outright dead. I'd hate to think what would happen to Georgeo. He never cared what the color of my skin was. It didn't matter to him that I was black and he was white. He was the only such person I had ever encountered. He was taking an awful risk just by being my friend.

I didn't say it, but that meant more to me than he'd ever really know.

As I laughed with exhilaration at my literary development, I leaned my head back against the tree that we were sitting under. As I did so, I noticed that the air had become warmer. One look at the sun stole the laughter right out of my mouth.

As if reading my mind, Georgeo plunged his hand into his shirt pocket and retrieved a large, brass-plated watch from it. He glanced at it for less than a second before scrambling to his feet. "Time to go! We're really late!" he exclaimed.

"Not again!" I cried as I leapt up from the grass.

It always seemed so bizarre to me. When I was out in the field, I would try and will the sun to go faster, to drift quickly across the blue sky and let us be done for the day. A few hours in the cotton took ages to pass, but a few hours with my best friend always flew by in the blink of an eye. Today was no different, and now I feared I would be late for the count.

Any minute now, Mr. Slate and Sam, his lackey, would be lining everyone up on the edge of the field for the morning count. It was their way of making sure everyone was still there. They didn't want any of their slaves trying to escape.

Georgeo and I sprinted as fast as we could through the thin edge of the forest that kept us hidden from the world. The temperature was rising as we went, causing a twinge of panic to race through me. I could not be late. I had cut it close a dozen times, but I had never been late for the count before. I wasn't sure what I feared more: the lash . . . or my father's disappointed glare.

I had to keep my lessons a secret from my family, just the same as anyone else. Georgeo had told me not to tell a soul. If one person had loose lips, a rumor like that would spread like wildfire, and I would be caught and punished. I loved my family more than anything, but I had to keep it from them, just in case.

Tree branches whipped lightly against my bare arms as I ran. The hot, moist air was rushing in and out of my lungs in large gasps as I bounded over fallen logs and moss-covered rocks. Sweat was already collecting on my forehead, causing the spectacles to slip down to the end of my nose. I slapped them back in place just as Georgeo and I came upon the fork in the path. This was where we always parted ways. This was where we sometimes shared a final joke or finished a final story. Today, however, there was no time for either.

For a brief second, we both paused at the fork, our chests heaving, and stared at one another. "Next week?" I asked.

Georgeo nodded, taking a few spry steps backward. "Yes! Now, go! Hurry!"

With a wide grin on my face, I dashed forward several yards. Maybe I could still make it on time.

"Isaac!" I heard from behind me. I skidded to a stop and whirled around at the sound of my name. Georgeo trotted over to where I stood, holding out his hand. "My spectacles!" he said.

I had nearly forgotten. Georgeo would always allow me to wear them while I was studying. He and I had the same problem with fuzzy eyesight. It didn't stop me from working or doing anything else, but when I had to focus on small words and sentences, I needed something to sharpen up my vision.

With a simultaneous laugh, we both jaunted off in separate directions again. It always took a few minutes for my brain to get used to my eyes seeing without the spectacles. I managed just fine without them, but I sure would have liked to have a pair of my very own. The entire world seemed a little bit clearer with them.

Now that there was a clear, defined path for me to follow, I could really turn on the speed. My legs had saved me plenty of times in the past, and I was counting on them to do the same today. I had to get back. I had to be there for the count. I wasn't about to be the reason for anyone to be punished. I couldn't bear the thought of anyone taking a blow from a whip because of something I did. That thought alone pushed me even faster.

The lush green forest was whizzing by me as I ran. Squirrels and chipmunks scattered in front of me, terrified at the sound of my feet pounding heavily on the dirt. In a matter of a few seconds, I had exploded out from the forest and into the cotton field. In the distance, I could make out a line of dark-skinned workers spread out just in front of the fields. Sam was doing the count.

No, no, no! I screamed in my mind. *Not yet!*

Chapter 2

I lowered my head and barreled forward, snatching lightning-fast handfuls of cotton as I went. The bushes were high, and I could remain hidden as long as I kept my head down and didn't kick up too much dust. It seemed to take an eternity to cross that field, grabbing as much warm, fluffy cotton as I could, but I finally managed to edge up behind Sam just as I heard him finish his count.

"One fifty-five?" he muttered to himself, sounding puzzled. He took a moment to scan the line of slaves, absentmindedly scratching his shin with his thumb. "Dawson," he said after a moment. "Isaac Dawson."

"Yes, sir?" I said, raising my head and showing my position just a few feet behind him. I was trying my best to hide my ragged breathing, but Sam noticed immediately.

"Where you been, boy?" he asked, looking me up and down.

I swallowed hard and shrugged my shoulder. "Nowhere, Mr. Sam. I've been right here working."

Sam narrowed his dark eyes at me. "Why're you all sweaty and out of breath?"

"It's 'cause I work hard for you, Mr. Sam. Real hard!" I said, doing my best to appear genuine. I turned and showed him the armful of cotton that I had plucked while running through the field. "See?"

Sam pursed his lips as he stared down at me. At that moment, I was suddenly terrified that he was going to explode with anger and demand to know what I'd really been doing. The sweat rolling off me now was more from my rattling nerves than it was from the heat. After a second, though, Sam just shrugged and turned back around to face the sound of hooves as Mr. Slate rode up to him on his horse.

"Everything in place?" Slate asked, his gravelly voice low and steady.

Sam took a big breath and stood as straight as he could. "Yes, Mr. Slate. No problems."

With nothing more than a curt nod, Slate dug his heels into the flank of his white horse and galloped away, leaving everyone to deflate and relax, including Sam.

"All right, then!" Sam shouted for all to hear. "Everyone get to work!"

Just the same as they did each morning, every slave started forward, sauntering into the fields and spreading out to cover as much ground as they could. I fell in with my family as they pushed into the cotton. I didn't have a sack yet, but I knew Pa would have grabbed it for me. Sure enough, as I approached him, I was relieved to see that he had.

"Thanks, Pa," I said, wrapping my hand around the rough, burlap bag. Pa held it tight, though, keeping me from taking it and forcing me to look up at him.

"Where were you?" he asked, his big brown eyes boring into me. His shining forehead creased heavily as his eyebrows pulled together. "I heard you leave real early this morning."

I blinked several times at his question, opening my mouth over and over, hoping some words would come out. "I just . . . I just went to see the animals in the woods and I . . . got a little lost." Even I was surprised by how well the fib sounded.

Pa reminded me an awful lot of Mr. Sam as he narrowed his eyes down at me. It was all I could do to keep from dropping my gaze to the ground. He shifted his jaw back and forth as he pondered over my response, making his thick, dark beard dance underneath his chin.

Finally, without a word, he released his grip on the cotton bag and gave a jerk of his head, signaling me to get to work. I had to swallow the excited giggle that threatened to burst out of my mouth. Just a few minutes ago, I was running for my life. I was seconds away from my secret being found out. I was terrified that I was going to lose my best friend. Now, everything was fine. I had gotten away with it. The secret was safe. With a hint of a smile on my lips, I opened the burlap sack and stuffed my armload of cotton inside.

"Where were you *really*?" a voice asked from behind me.

I felt a spark run through as I turned around. The voice had startled me, but I immediately relaxed as soon as I saw that it had come from my older brother.

"Like I told Pa," I said to him. "I was looking at the critters in the woods and got lost, Samuel. No big mystery."

Samuel nodded, his eyes flicking back and forth between mine. "You're lyin'."

His declaratory statement caught me off guard. I froze for a moment, my face contorted into a look of alarm for a brief second before I consciously smoothed it out. "I am not," I insisted. "You'd best hush up now and get working before we both catch a whippin'."

Samuel snickered and released his scrutinizing gaze. "Fine. I know you're lying, though. Can't fool me, Isaac."

I shook my head and bent to pluck a handful of cotton from the nearest shrub, watching him walk away from the corner of my eye. I don't know how, but Samuel always had a knack for being able to tell when someone was lying. It was a pretty remarkable talent for a boy only twelve years old, but to this day I have never seen him guess wrong. I had so far been able to keep him from finding out my secret, but I was slipping. My fib about the critters in the forest had been so convincing that even Pa hadn't questioned it. Samuel, though . . . Samuel always knew. I would have to be more careful around him from now on.

The morning drew ever onward, nudging the sun higher up into the sky. The heat was starting to take its toll. Plenty of the workers were slowing down. As I made my way from bush to bush, I began to overhear one of my fellow slaves trying to convince a friend of his to keep moving.

"Come on, Nate. Don't go quittin' on me," Elijah said. He was relatively young, very lean and muscular from constant working. His friend—Nate—was a bit older, judging by the thick streaks of grey in his hair, and the heat was getting to him pretty good. He was shuffling lazily along the rows of bushes, sluggishly grabbing a few handfuls of the white fibers that kept us all alive.

"You remember what happened to the last fella that came back with a bag half-full," the man continued. "Don't let 'em see you draggin' your feet!"

"I can't," Nate wheezed, his cheeks puffing out with each exhale. "Too hot. I'm not feeling so good. I'm . . . feelin' dizzy."

"I know," Elijah said. "Here, let me see your bag."

After glancing around a few times to make sure that neither Slate nor Mr. Sam was in the vicinity, Elijah dropped his sack of cotton onto the dry ground and opened it up. As I watched, he began taking out large handfuls of cotton, stuffing them into Nate's bag and filling it considerably. Nate simply nodded in acceptance, patting his friend on the back to thank him.

I couldn't help but smile as I watched them. I was filled with pride at the sight. There we all were, in the worst state of life that we could have ever found ourselves in, and we still found the goodness to help each other out. Each one of us knew that the man or woman next to us was in the exact same boat as we were. We were all in this together. Pa would sometimes say that the workers in the field were better people than the ones running the country. At the time, I was sure he was right. After all, in front of my eyes, I had just seen a man help another man, simply because he knew that Nate would have done the same thing for him if the roles had been reversed.

"Don't you worry," I said to them in a hushed voice. "The water should be coming soon."

A few times throughout the day, a handful of the house workers, usually women or teenage girls, would venture into the fields carrying buckets of water to keep us from drying out. It was just about the only thing we had to look forward to, and it was the closest thing we would get to being allowed a break. The women would come out, and everyone would slowly percolate in from the fields to come and take a long, slow drink. Most times, the water was cool and refreshing. It was never enough, though. In the heat, you'd sweat just as much as those buckets could hold, and everyone who was able would stand around the water spigot in the evenings, drinking in all they could. As luck would have it, I spotted a few of the women coming into the fields, each of them carrying a large bucket of water.

They scuttled gingerly into the cotton, careful not to spill any. If they came back with wet or dirty clothes, they knew they'd surely take a beating for it. They also knew they only had to come about a dozen yards in, and the workers would all flock to them like ants on honey. Sure enough, from all over the fields, they came, relishing the reprieve.

"Isaac, freeze tag!" my sister shouted at me. I barely had time to register her words before she was practically on top of me. Fortunately, my quickness saved me once again and I dodged to the side as she stumbled past me, slipping on the loose soil and toppling to the ground.

From a few feet away, Pa called out to her. "Felicia, you all right?"

From the ground, Felicia rolled onto her back and slowly sat up. "Yeah, Pa!" she shouted back, slapping the dirt from her long, skinny legs and shaking out her head full of short braids.

Pa shook his head as he continued forward. "That girl, worryin' me all the time, I tell you . . ." he muttered.

I tried to stifle my laughter as I helped Felicia to her feet, but it spilled past my lips. "You shush up, Isaac!" she barked at me.

Felicia was always falling down, tripping over something, or running into something else. She was always cleaning a scrape on her knobby knee or pulling something or another out of her braids. She was the clumsiest person I had ever seen, but it gave all of us something to laugh at, and a reason to smile was always welcome among us workers. Besides, Felicia always ended up okay. It took an awful lot to hurt that girl.

We took our time drinking the water. It was cool and delicious, and it helped soothe the ache on our tongues. In addition, it was the only time we were allowed to pause in our work. Naturally, we would try to draw it out as long as we could. Today, as I was splashing some of the water on my head and letting it seep into my thick mane of hair, I became aware of Master Tomstin himself, in the middle of a conversation with an unfamiliar man in a horse-drawn carriage. My brain suddenly bellowed loudly at me, telling me to turn away and get back to the others before Tomstin discovered I was there, but my curiosity was even stronger, rooting me in place once I heard what they were speaking about.

"I personally wonder why those Yankees are so set on freeing the black man," Master Tomstin was saying, turning to look out on his beloved fields. "I am positive that the country would halt in its tracks without the things we provide. Why, the cotton from this very field is the same cotton that they use in the nation's capital to keep them warm at night. Why even the cotton for their clothes, their bed sheets, their towels . . . it all comes from places just like ours, Mr. Kin. They'd do well to realize that, in my opinion. Besides, without me, all these workers would be homeless, living in the woods and back alleys like vermin.

I do them a service, and they simply return the favor."

Mr. Kin, the man in the wagon, who was heavyset and white-haired, fanned himself with the collar of his jacket. In his other hand, his thick fingers gripped a large glass of dark brown liquid. "Oh, yes, Jefferson. You are a true saint, indeed."

I couldn't believe my ears. The sarcasm was obvious in Mr. Kin's voice. I had never heard anyone speak to Master Tomstin like that. I was suddenly more engrossed than ever.

"Don't you worry yourself," Mr. Kin went on. "Soon, this war will be over, the South will prevail as we all knew they would, and you can continue on with your . . . greatness . . . without any interruption."

Master Tomstin scoffed and shook his head, looking up at Mr. Kin with an odd expression on his face, as if he were studying the man. "You're a smug one, aren't you?"

Mr. Kin let out a low, rumbling laugh. "That I am, Jefferson. Just be glad those Union boys don't come down this far. They'd string us both up for sure. You, especially."

Master Tomstin squinted his eyes slightly and allowed a smirk to pull at his lips. "Indeed. Tell me, Mr. Kin, how many slaves do you have in your fields?"

Mr. Kin barked out a laugh that jiggled his entire torso. "I don't count anymore. Could be ten, could be ten thousand. Who knows?"

"*You* should," Tomstin responded sharply. "Or has the drink blurred your mind?"

Mr. Kin smiled widely. "So it would seem."

Master Tomstin shook his head again and leaned casually against the door of the carriage, turning his back to me. "You know, Mr. Kin . . . I was worried about our meeting today. But, now that I have met my *competition,* I do believe I will sleep soundly tonight."

"Is that so?" Mr. Kin asked, seeming only amused.

"It is," Master Tomstin said, his voice suddenly cold. "You're no competition at all. You're nothing more than a shell of a man hiding in a whiskey bottle, can't see what's going on in the world around you. You're nothing but a waste, sir."

Mr. Kin smiled widely and raised his glass. "Here, here, I'll drink to that."

Master Tomstin pushed himself away from the carriage and glared at his fellow plantation owner. "Mr. Kin, I do believe it's time you got yourself home. Don't forget to collect your effects from my estate."

Mr. Kin nodded. "I agree, sir. Driver!"

With a loud crack, the wagon's horses let out a startled whinny and lurched forward, jarring

Mr. Kin in his seat and nearly making him spill his drink.

"Good day, Jefferson!" he slurred.

Master Tomstin waited until the wagon had rattled a good distance away before replying. "And to you," he muttered.

I couldn't help but think, as the wagon rumbled up toward the house, that Master Tomstin really did find Mr. Kin worthless if he was letting the man near his home without caring to accompany him. As he pulled a handkerchief from his pocket, he ran it across his forehead before turning toward the field.

Immediately, I finished my water and shuffled back to the others, not keen on being caught listening in. I got one more mouthful of water and then hurried back to work, making sure to stick near my father to avoid suspicion. From my peripheral vision, I saw Master Tomstin make his way to the edge of the field, where he propped himself against a wooden fencepost and peered out over all the workers, his eyes focusing intently on something I couldn't see. Beside me, my father and his friend Blue began speaking in hushed tones. Since I was already on an eavesdropping spree, I didn't even try to tune it out.

"Seems to me Master Tomstin been spendin' a lot of time down here," Blue murmured.

Furtively, Pa raised his eyes to sneak a glance at Tomstin. "Yeah, I guess. Probably just makin' sure we bustin' our backs."

"Nah," Blue dismissed. "That's what he pays Mr. Slate for, ain't it?"

Pa cracked a smile, but didn't take his eyes off his work, his experienced fingers deftly separating cotton bolls from the plants. "Well," he said. "If I owned this place, I'd be watchin' us, too. 'Specially you."

The two men shared a quiet laugh. "Yeah," Blue said with a sigh. "Wouldn't that be a sight? Ole Duke Dawson up there in that big ol' house."

Pa nodded. "Yep. Quite a sight, sure enough it be."

"I don't think you're catching what I'm saying," Blue said, more serious this time. "Master Tomstin's been watchin', but . . . it ain't us he's watchin'."

Pa's eyebrows began to crease in confusion. "What you talkin' about?"

"See for yourself," Blue muttered to the ground.

Just like Pa, I couldn't help but raise my eyes and glance over at Tomstin, who was still focused on the same thing from a few moments ago. Following his gaze, I peered over to the spot Tomstin was staring at. Unsettlingly, my eyes fell upon Felicia as she stopped to stand straight and stretch her back. Tomstin was staring at my sister. I didn't know exactly why, but I knew I didn't like it.

"How old is Felicia, now?" Blue asked.

My father took a deep breath and let it out slowly. "She just turned thirteen, I do believe."

"That's just how old *my* daughter was when Master Tomstin picked her to work in-house. She spent two years up there, scrubbin', cookin', and cleanin' for that man. When she finally came back, she wasn't the same. Some part of her was . . . gone."

Pa was still staring over at Felicia. "What do you mean?" he asked.

Blue shrugged. "She ain't never said, and I don't ask. I don't think I want to know what all happened in that house. To tell you the truth, I don't think I could take it. But, you better believe . . . if he picks Felicia, she'll have to go up there to suffer the same thing. Ain't nothin' you can do, Duke. Nothin' any of us can do."

My father's face mirrored my own. His forehead was suddenly covered in deep wrinkles. I could see veins bulging on top his bald head, too. Even his beard was working back and forth in concern. I had no beard, and my hair was much bushier, but I had the same worry on my face. I didn't care for the things Blue was saying any more than Pa did. Unfortunately, like the man had said, there was nothing anyone could do about it.

The last couple of hours of the day passed just as slowly as on any other day. By the time it was late afternoon, most of the workers were tired and worn out, aching to get back to their shacks and cabins so that they could lie down. There was still plenty of daylight left, though, and the kids would always use that time to get in some much-needed play. It was the best way to forget about the stress of the day, and also the best way to keep from dreading tomorrow, which we knew would be filled with more work.

Freeze tag was our favorite game. Perhaps it was because we didn't know any others, but we would play freeze tag almost every day after work. It was the only time we had to unwind, and was also just about the only time we got to spend with other kids.

My favorite of the other children was a young boy named Munroe. He was my age, about ten years old, or so, but his skin was a shade darker and he was a little bit rounder than I was. No one was quite sure how he was able to put on extra weight, really. He would insist it was just baby fat, but it was still fun to play tag with him. He was an easy target. On the other hand, he might have been the cleverest of us. After all, he would only chase groups of girls.

As Samuel and I made our way in from the fields, he suddenly stopped and slapped me hard on the arm. "You're it!" he shouted before turning and sprinting into the woods on the back side of the slave cabins. On the other side of this narrow patch of forest was Master Tomstin's house, so we would always be careful enough to keep our distance.

For several yards, I chased after him, both of us gleefully. We hopped over sticks and ducked under low branches, weaving in and out of the thin tree trunks as I tried to outmaneuver him. After just a minute, though, we heard something that stopped us both, effectively putting an end to our game.

"What shall we do with a drunken sailor? What shall we do with a drunken sailor early in the morning?"

Someone was trying to sing. The words were loud and nearly indecipherable, but the voice belonged to an adult man, which was troubling. It didn't sound like Tomstin, so we naturally had to move in closer to investigate. We tiptoed through the thin underbrush, trying to make as little noise as possible. It took only a few seconds to come upon the source of the awful singing. For some reason, it didn't surprise me.

Mr. Kin, the fat, slurring plantation owner whom I had seen earlier in the day was now in the woods outside of Tomstin's house, swaying from side to side, his head tilted back in ecstasy as he absentmindedly sprayed urine in front of him. Through the trees, I could see his carriage parked on the road, waiting. Why he chose the forest instead of the outhouse by Tomstin's manor, I just don't know. Samuel and I crept up until we were just a few feet away from him. We concealed ourselves behind a thick bramble bush, watching with amusement as Mr. Kin continued singing.

"Put him in the bilge and make him drink it! Put him in the bilge and make him drink it early in the morning!"

As we watched, though, Samuel elbowed me in the shoulder and pointed to the ground in front of our hiding bush. There, slithering through the loose leaves and twigs, a rattlesnake stealthily approached Mr. Kin, who still didn't even know that we were there. If he didn't move, things were not going to end well for him. I didn't know Mr. Kin, but I did know he was a plantation owner. A slave owner. Part of me wanted to warn him, but . . . another part of me wanted to see him bitten. If Tomstin was the one on the receiving end of a venomous snake, I sure wouldn't feel any remorse whatsoever. Why should this fellow be any different? I watched the snake closing in on him, slithering closer and closer. I watched the serpent coil its body, my eyes wide with anticipation. The part of me that wished Mr. Kin harm was about to be very satisfied. Once the rattle started, I knew it was all over.

With blinding speed, the snake lunged at a stunned Mr. Kin.

I gasped.

Mr. Kin had not been bitten. Instead, Samuel's hand was there, clamped around the snake's neck, just behind its head. I hadn't noticed him slip out from behind our bush. I had been too focused on the snake. As soon as Samuel stood up with the reptile in his hands, Kin spun around, shouting loudly as his eyes fell upon the snake.

"Good heavens!" he panted, clutching his chest.

"This here devil snake almost had you for sure, Mister," Samuel replied. "If I hadn't grabbed him up, you'd be a goner."

Mr. Kin looked down at the rattler. "Devil snake, you say?"

Samuel nodded. "Yessir. Just look in his eyes. He ain't got no soul. Here, look." He lifted the snake up toward Mr. Kin's face, which was almost enough to put the man on his back. He stumbled back a step before catching himself.

Laughing, Samuel wound up his arm and hurled the snake far into the trees before turning around. "Be careful in here, Mister," he said, taking a step back toward me.

I ducked down to avoid detection, peering through the tangled branches of the bush to watch Kin waddle after my brother. "Hold on here just a minute!" Mr. Kin called out.

With his eyebrows raised, Samuel rubbed his bald head and turned around. "Yeah?"

"Why boy, you just saved my life," Mr. Kin said somberly, bending down to look at Samuel. "A life that I regret to say . . . many would consider not worth saving."

Though I knew nothing about this man, I was sure this was true.

"Don't worry," Samuel said nonchalantly. "You woulda done the same thing for me. Right?"

Mr. Kin looked taken aback by the question. His flabby neck quivered as he tried to open his mouth and form a response. "Well, I—I . . . I certainly would have. We—we Southern gentlemen are a . . . fine upstanding breed. Of course! I would have done the same thing for you, young man."

Samuel leaned in close, his gaze boring into Mr. Kin's beady eyes. Mr. Kin looked rather bewildered, but he couldn't seem to look away. I knew what Samuel was doing. He'd given me that same look just this morning after I'd come back from my lesson with Georgeo. After a moment, he let out a sigh.

"No, sir . . . you wouldn't have," he said. Turning to leave, he gave Mr. Kin a nod. "I gotta get goin'. See ya around."

"What's your name?" Mr. Kin asked, pulling a shining metal flash from his jacket pocket.

"Samuel," my brother replied, giving me a nod to join him as we headed back toward the cabins.

From behind us, I heard Mr. Kin exhale. "Well . . . thank you, Samuel. Your valor will not be forgotten, at least not by me" he said softly.

Once we were out of sight of Mr. Kin, Samuel and I took off at a run, hurrying to get out of the forest before anyone else saw us there. It wasn't long before we burst back out by the cabins, our faces slick with sweat again.

The rest of the children were all engrossed in their game of tag. No one noticed us emerge from the woods. We took a moment to compose ourselves and then joined in, not eager to explain where we'd been. What had just happened was unusual, but still not quite interesting enough to merit a retelling, in my opinion. Samuel might, though, if just to brag about saving a man from a snake bite. Sure enough, as he approached a group of older kids, I heard him whispering the story to them.

"Gonna getcha, Isaac!" Felicia shouted, charging at me. Her short braids bounced with each step as she giggled her way toward me. Firing my leg muscles, I quickly spun away and out of her reach. As I said before, though, I was known for my speed . . . just as Felicia was known for her clumsiness. As she swung her hand around to where I had just been, the movement threw her off balance and she toppled to the ground, using her momentum to roll right back to her feet as if nothing had happened. She was resilient, I couldn't deny.

The late afternoon was the best time for us. The sun was dying out, leaving the air a bit cooler and more enjoyable. While the adults relaxed and conversed amongst themselves, this was the only time we had to be kids. We had to cram all the wonders of childhood into just a few hours each evening. We made the best of it, though. We always found a way to smile and laugh off the pressures and the injustices of the day. That was the key. Being a slave was a terrible way to live your life, but it was the only life we knew. If we'd had any inkling on the things we were missing out on, I think smiling and laughing would have been a lot more difficult. We were blissful in our ignorance as we ran and played, and I believe that's just how Master Tomstin preferred it.

From the road, we heard the familiar rattling of Tomstin's wagon approaching. We all ceased our playing and lowered our gaze. On occasion, if Master Tomstin was feeling particularly mean, he might pull out a switch just for seeing someone having too much fun. He'd done it before. None of us wanted to take that chance.

As the wagon passed by us on the narrow dirt road, I noticed that Georgeo was in the passenger side of the wagon, wearing the same outfit he'd been wearing by the river this morning. He caught my eye and gave a smile, which I returned momentarily before flattening my expression once again. Tomstin hadn't noticed, though, he was smiling at someone, too. As he tipped his hat, I saw that he was once again looking at Felicia.

Just as before, I felt my eyebrows furrowing in concern as I remembered Blue's warning to my father. I didn't want Felicia to be taken away up to the house. I didn't want her to be gone for two years. My head spun around, trying to find the shack that my family called home. As my eyes fell upon it, I saw Pa standing just outside the door, watching the carriage make its way down the narrow dirt road. I knew he had seen Tomstin's gesture, too, and I knew he was thinking the same things I was. Unfortunately, as Blue had also said, there was nothing that could be done about it.

As the evening progressed into darkness, all of us kids gradually made our way back to our families, back to our shacks or cabins. For the Dawsons, it was a peaceful time of day, but one that was also predictable. Every night like clockwork, as the crickets were coming to life and the moon was making its first appearance, my family would gather together in the small, cramped room of our cabin, holding hands and saying our prayers. By the tiny hearth, we would all join together and bow our heads. Tonight was no different.

"Everyone holdin' hands?" Pa asked.

We all nodded.

"Good," he said, looking over to Ma, whose long hair was still tied up in a bun. I did think this was a bit odd, as she usually couldn't wait to take it down and let it flow freely down her back. With it tied up, she still looked like she was ready for work. "Sometimes, a touch of a hand is all a person needs." Pa went on. "Lots of comfort to be had, just in the touch of someone who cares. It's how we know we ain't alone in the world. It's how we know . . . even in the most troubling of times . . . that everything's gonna be all right. You hear me now?"

"Yes, sir," said the three of us together.

With a minute smile and nod, Pa looked over to Ma. "Tonight," he whispered to her, his eyes strangely misty.

Ma nodded in return and lowered her head. I had the feeling that she was getting teary-eyed, too. Felicia, Samuel and I exchanged puzzled glances, but said nothing. We knew better than to interrupt our father during prayer time.

"You kids," Pa said, staring intently at us. His voice was unusually soft. "You gotta know there's nothin' in this world that me and your Ma wouldn't do for you. You also need to know that . . . there's nothin' stronger than a family's bond. Nothin'. Whether we in the room or . . . spread out across the land. We are still a family.

Nothin' is more powerful than that. Mama, lead us in a prayer now."

Ma nodded. Everyone bowed their head . . . except me. "Dear Lord up above," Ma said quietly, her voice wavering. "Please . . . protect and watch over this family. Please, take care of our children. They will need Your guidance."

As Ma continued with the prayer, the wetness in my father's eyes was becoming obvious. As it spilled down his cheeks, I couldn't help but feel the slightest bit worried. My father was the strongest, sturdiest, most reliable man I knew. He was definitely the hardest worker I had ever seen. He was a plantation owner's dream. My mother was a close second. To see them both breaking down like that, it was disconcerting to me. I had never seen it before. It was the first time I had seen my father shed a tear at all. As I glanced furtively over to Felicia and Samuel, I saw that they seemed just as surprised and confused as I was.

Now that I thought about it, for the last few days, I had noticed my father becoming more sullen, more withdrawn, like the weight of the world had suddenly decided to take a ride on his shoulders. He had never been that way before. He was always helping us along, teaching us to see the bright spots in life, even on the darkest days. Samuel and I had wondered if it was the talk of the war that was finally getting to him. For a couple of years, it seemed the war had been raging on, but it had never affected Pa like this. Perhaps it was because there were rumors of an end in sight, a Southern victory that would keep us all as slaves forever. I had heard my mother and father talking once or twice about their wish for freedom, for our family to never again fear for our lives over a few pounds of cotton. Maybe that's what had been worrying him. Truthfully, I didn't know for sure, and I wasn't about to question him about it. If he wanted me to know what was going on in his head, I trusted that he would tell me.

Until then, all I could do was worry.

Chapter 3

For a long time that night, I lay awake in my bed, staring up at the thick shadows that pooled in the empty ceiling of the cabin. I knew I should be asleep. The morning always came far too early, and I knew what might happen if I wasn't working fast enough. Even so, I couldn't seem to close my eyes. There was an odd feeling in the air that wouldn't quite allow me to relax.

It rolled over me in my bunk, setting my fingers and toes to twitching. I had no idea why, but I felt almost nervous, like something was different or something was about to change. I had only a few minutes to dwell on this strange thought before I heard a faint creaking on the old wooden floor behind me. Intrigued, I propped myself up on one elbow and searched the darkened room for the source of the noise.

On the floor of the cabin, my father crouched on one knee, his face tensed with concentration as he reached down to grasp one of the weathered wooden floorboards. Despite his efforts to make it subtle, the board gave a loud, high-pitched squeak as the nails were torn, pulled up from the frame. Samuel and Felicia stirred in their beds, but remained silent. Perhaps, like me, they were simply observing, hoping to learn what was going on.

I watched quietly as Pa set the board to the side and leaned over the rectangular hole he had just created. Before I could wonder what he was doing, he reached his hand into the hole and withdrew something from the blackness. Even in the dim light of the cabin, I could tell that it was an old tin box, decorated with a picture of something I couldn't make out. Hurriedly, Pa opened the box with a tiny popping sound and pulled out what appeared to be a piece of folded paper. He stared at it for a few seconds, opening it and scanning the inside before tucking it in the pocket of his wool trousers. As soon as he had stashed the paper, he moved to Felicia's bed, shaking her awake.

"Come on, now!" he said in an urgent whisper. "Everybody up! Wake up!" He nudged Samuel on the shoulder. The tone of his voice was enough to put me on edge as I sat up in bed. "You, too!" he said to me. "Everybody get dressed! We don't have much time!"

"Time for what? What is it?" Samuel asked, his voice still thick and groggy.

Felicia was the first to vacate her bed. "What's going on?" she asked sternly.

As I slipped my feet down onto the rough wooden floor, I heard a small whimper coming from the front of the cabin. While Pa gathered clothes and belongings for Samuel and Felicia, I saw Ma pacing in a short line by the door. She was largely obscured by shadows, but I could see that she had her arms wrapped tightly around her midsection, and one hand clamped over her mouth to stifle the sobs that were shaking her body. Her sallow cheeks were wet with tears.

Something was wrong.

Upon seeing me staring at her in confusion, she removed the hand from her mouth and snapped her fingers. "You listen to your father!" she urged, using the same hushed tone of voice. "Get yourselves dressed and don't argue!"

She shuffled forward, seizing the first cotton shirt that she could find and slipped it over my head. "Quickly. Now," she muttered.

In my state of bewilderment, I couldn't find any words to voice my distress. Just what was happening? I felt something was definitely wrong. I was feeling an intense worry tumbling around the pit of my stomach, but I could only obey my parents. I trusted them. Rather than ask questions that would anger Pa, I simply hitched up my trousers and waited for the next set of instructions. Felicia and Samuel had also realized that arguing was going to get them nowhere. In a few seconds, they were both fully dressed and Pa was ushering all of us toward the front where Ma stood peeking through the cracked door.

"Anything?" Pa asked.

Ma shook her head. "Nothing."

Slowly, Pa eased the door open and stepped out into the muggy night air. He whipped his head from side to side, searching the rows of cabins for something. After a moment, he turned around and gave us all a nod.

"Come on!" Ma hissed, dragging us out the door. She took Pa's hand and grasped Felicia's with the other. Felicia seized a hold of Samuel, who clutched onto my hand as he went, turning us into a linked chain as we glided through the quarter houses. The three of us kept deathly silent, even going so far as to jog on our tiptoes to keep from making loud footfalls. We knew we were not supposed to be out at night. We were warned daily of the punishment we would face if we were out past curfew. If we were caught, we'd all be caned fiercely. The fear of that torment was enough to keep us quiet. Part of me wanted to turn and run back to the cabin, to sprint back to safety, just to ensure that I wouldn't get into trouble. Instead, however, I kept going, my eyes focused on Pa's heels as he pulled all of us into the field. I had never been in the field after dark. It felt so different in the moonlight, much less welcoming. I had no choice but to swallow my discomfort and continue on.

Grasshoppers leapt out of our path in every direction, some of them bouncing off of us as we went. The night insects were loud and repetitive, helping to cover the sounds of our movement. Ma and Pa ran with their heads lowered and their shoulders hunched. The cotton reached up to my neck, but to them, it was only waist-high. They were trying not to be seen. As we reached the end of the massive field, it occurred to me that we were running away. We were escaping the plantation.

Over the years, I'd heard stories of runaway slaves, a once-in-a-blue-moon brave man or woman that would sneak away and make a mad dash for freedom to one of the Northern states. Many of them were caught, brought back and whipped mercilessly until the fight had bled out of them. A few were chased down by the Boss's men, a few came back with gunshot wounds, and a few never came back at all. I don't know what Pa was thinking, but as we crossed into the thick forest tree line, I knew we'd come too far to go back now.

The forest was even darker and more ominous than I'd imagined. I'd been through this area before in my morning lessons with Georgeo, but just like the field, it took on a new life in the darkness. The sounds of animals and insects were louder, more condensed, and my skin shuddered as I felt their eyes on me. I clutched Samuel's hand tight, making sure I wouldn't slip loose and be left behind. I couldn't even imagine being lost in these woods alone.

Loose twigs and leaf litter tumbled around our ankles as we plodded through the dense growth. My trousers, which were too big to begin with, were getting snagged and caught on every thorn and jagged stone that I passed. It felt like the forest was trying to reach out and take me, keep me tangled within it until the patrollers found me and dragged me back to the plantation. All I could do was follow Pa as he dragged us all along behind him.

As a group, we scurried. We scrambled through the forest for what seemed like ages. In reality, it couldn't have been more than an hour or two, but we must have traveled miles. We hiked over hills, splashed through streams and creeks, all following Pa, who forged on like the fires of Hades were burning inside him. My feet were aching badly. Working in the field all day was one thing, but hiking, running, and climbing—that was something different entirely! I was going to have blisters for sure. Finally, Felicia was able to catch her breath enough to ask what we were all thinking.

"Where are we going, Pa?" she asked, sounding slightly annoyed. She received no answer. Pa's only reply was his heavy footsteps on the forest floor. Realizing that asking again would be fruitless, Felicia fell silent.

The five of us trudged onward, panting and gasping for breath. Through the occasional breaks in the wooded canopy, the cool, silver moonlight would spill through and I could see my father leading the way, his dark skin glistening with a sheen of sweat. He seemed to know exactly where he was going. How could he? How many times had he made this journey by himself before tonight? Where was he taking us?

I didn't have to wait long to find out.

All at once, the forest ended, and we tumbled out into the open air once more. The trees had given way to a large, empty field of tall grass. We pushed our way through for a few more paces until Pa hunkered down in front of us. Wordlessly, we all followed his lead. His eyes were trained on something up ahead, and as I craned my neck to see over the grass, I spotted the thing he was focused on.

About one hundred yards from where we crouched in the grass, a set of train tracks glistened serenely in the moonlight. In the distance, the faint rumble of an approaching train could be heard.

"We're running away, aren't we?" Felicia asked.

For the first time since we left the cabin, Pa turned to face us. His eyes were wide and urgent, and his voice was deep and grave. "Yes," he replied. "You're gonna catch this train, and it's gonna take you North to Reading."

Felicia blinked at him. "Reading?"

"Reading, Pennsylvania," Pa clarified.

I stared around Pa's broad shoulder. We were going to hop a train? How were we going to do that? It's not like the conductor would stop and pick up five runaway slaves.

"Hold on," Felicia said, her voice full of concern. "You said 'you.' You mean 'us,' don't you?"

She was right. I hadn't even noticed when he'd said it, but he had. My heartbeat immediately began to pick up again. What was going on? Why would he say that?

Ma and Pa exchanged glances before turning back to us.

"You mean 'us,' don't you, Pa?" Felicia pressed, her panic making her voice rise in pitch.

"No," Ma answered quietly. "Just you and your brothers, dear."

Samuel's hand tightened around mine.

"What?" Felicia cried. "No! No, we're not going without you!"

"You have to go," Pa told her, his face creased with sadness. I couldn't comprehend why he would be saying such things. Why would he bring us here only to abandon us?

Felicia continued to protest, sounding angry as she argued with our parents. "Not without you, Mama! I won't! None of us will!" Her words mirrored the things bubbling in my chest.

Ma reached out to Felicia and caressed her face. Her round cheek fit perfectly in the palm of Ma's hand. "Hush, child. Hush, now."

My mother's touch disintegrated Felicia's anger, and she burst into tears, clutching at Ma's dress. Seeing her so distraught was putting a lump in my own throat. Was this really happening? In the distance, the train's whistle grew a bit louder. It was a strange time to think it, but it suddenly occurred to me that I had never seen a train up close before, and now I was being told to jump onto one.

"I don't wanna go without you," Felicia sobbed.

"You know Master Tomstin," Ma said soothingly. "To lose a couple of kids from the field will surely upset him, but it ain't gonna do him much harm. Now, your father and I are the best workers on that plantation. If he found us missing, he'd come after us with everything he's got. You wouldn't be safe with us, baby."

Still in tears, Felicia could only shake her head. "I won't go . . . I won't go," she whimpered. I couldn't stop my own tears from falling now. I didn't like seeing my sister so upset, and the things my parents were saying only confused and frightened me.

Ahead of me, Samuel sniffled. "No, Ma! No, Pa! Don't!"

The train was growing ever closer, a colossal metal beast that barreled through the night, and my father's urgency was becoming even more palpable. "You mind me, now!" he growled. "All of you! You are gonna get on that train and you are gonna go and find a better life, you hear?" He turned to Felicia. "I ain't gonna watch you grow up in a cotton field, working your fingers to the bone every day for *nothing*! None of you are gonna grow up like that! Not if I can help it! This is your way out!" He was fighting the sorrow in his voice, but the wetness in his eyes betrayed him.

"This is all I can give you," he said somberly, looking around at all of us. "Now, I need you all to be brave, hear? It's time to go. Be brave for me."

With tears streaming down all of our faces, he stretched out his arms and pulled all of us together, all five of us, into one hug. It occurred to me that it was likely to be our last hug as a family. The thought terrified me, causing a loud sob to rip its way out of my throat. I squeezed his sinewy forearm with everything I had, not wanting to release it. After a moment, Pa let us go and turned to Felicia once more, giving her a strong hug before cradling her face gently in his calloused hands.

"You take care of them boys," he told her solemnly. "You watch out for 'em, hear?"

Felicia whimpered. "What if I don't know what to do?"

Pa shook his head. "That ain't gonna happen. You'll know what to do. I'm sure of it."

"But, what if I don't, Pa?" Felicia cried.

Ma inched forward on her knees, her face wet with still-flowing tears. "I'll be right there with you, child," she whispered. She placed her hand over her heart and patted her chest. "I can feel you in here. I always do. A mother can feel her babies even if they ain't around, you hear what I'm telling you?"

Felicia sniffled loudly before nodding.

"Good," Ma went on, a tiny smile trying to emerge on her lips. "If you're ever lost, or . . . feeling unsure, just tell me. Just tell it to the wind. Ask the wind what to do, and as sure as I'm hearing you right now, I will hear you then. You just have to listen for me. Just listen for me and believe, you understand?"

I couldn't comprehend what my mother was saying. I wondered if Felicia really understood it. I could only seem to focus on the train, the light of which was now piercing the veil of night that covered the landscape. I was almost hypnotized by it. I wanted to see what it looked like. I wanted to see the wheels and the smokestack. I wanted to see the cars and the cargo. I don't know if I was just looking for something to take my mind off of the sadness around me, but I continued to stare across the waving grass at the coming train. It rumbled closer and closer and I began to feel the dirt itself vibrating underneath me. It was so powerful. I was filled with fear and excitement all at once.

"Here," Pa said, bringing my attention back to my family. "Take this."

The pamphlet that he had pulled from beneath our cabin floor was thrust into Felicia's trembling hands. Felicia couldn't read what it said, but even in the dark, with my fuzzy eyesight, I could make out the print on the paper cover: 4-14 TO READING, PA.

"It's time," Pa said pointedly.

None of us argued this time. I think we had realized the pointless nature of it. Still, it didn't stop us from hating it. It didn't stop the tears that squeezed their way out of our shut eyelids.

One by one, Pa gave us a final, hurried embrace. As his arms closed around me, I tried to memorize everything about him: his beard, his shining head, the smell of dirt and sweat and cotton that lingered on his clothes. I tried to take mental photographs of everything, just so I would have something to look back and remember when he was gone. His hug was quick but powerful, and my small fingers could only grip feebly at his shoulder blades. Before I knew it, he had pulled away and was focusing on the approaching train. I had to fight the urge to lunge forward and latch onto him. Maybe then, he would be forced to come with us.

"Go!" he shouted back at us, almost bouncing on his hips. "You ride that train to freedom, and you don't *ever* look back! You hear me? It's time! You need to go, now!"

None of us moved. The only thing we could do was sob and cry at the situation. If nobody ran for the train, then our parents would have no choice but to return to the plantation with us and we would all be able to stay together. I think my father knew it, though. He knew we were thinking it, so he did the only thing he knew to do.

With a spark of mad rage in his eye, he turned and screamed right in our faces. "You get out of here! All of you!" he shouted. "Go NOW!"

That did the trick. Terrified, the three of us sprang simultaneously from our hiding spot and began sprinting toward the railroad tracks, our teary eyes locked on the oncoming train. The tall grass made progress difficult, though. My legs were so short that I had quite a time running through that mess, doing my best to keep from tripping and slamming my face into the ground.

As we neared the tracks, I saw that the train was even bigger than I had imagined. It seemed like some kind of colossal, serpentine demon that had escaped the Devil's clutches to come screaming and speeding across the countryside. Every blast of the horn was a bellowing roar that shook the very bones inside me. How on earth were we supposed to climb aboard that thing?

Just as the nose of the great beast was a few yards away from us, Felicia stopped in her tracks and turned back to us. "Get down!" she squealed, dropping suddenly into the grass. Samuel and I had no choice but to follow suit and dive into the tall green blades beside her. The engine of the train sped right by us, black smoke erupting steadily from atop it. As soon as it had passed— and the conductor could no longer see us— Felicia pushed herself to her feet once more.

"Come on!" she shouted at us, waving her arm for us to follow.

We did so without question. The tall grass ended after a few more feet, and there was only a solid layer of rock gravel beside the tracks. That would make it easier to move, but that still didn't help us to actually get *on* the train.

If I said being that close to such a tremendous machine didn't scare the daylights out of me, I'd be lying. My feet wanted to turn and run the other way, to escape the path of the angry beast and get to safety. If either my brother or sister had fled, I would have surely followed.

Fortunately, they both stayed . . . and I stayed with them.

In front of me, Felicia reached out for a railing to grab a hold of, but it whipped by at an impossible speed. She tried a second time, but the train was simply moving too fast.

As we stood there, the boxcars thundered past us one by one, taking our opportunities of escape with them. Our time to act was rapidly dwindling. I began to feel a thick, black dread settle in the back of my skull. This wasn't going to work. We weren't going to make it.

All at once, as if reading my mind, Samuel exploded into action beside me. He took off at a dead sprint in the same direction the train was going, hurrying as quickly as he could.

"Come on!" he called back to us, his feet kicking up gravel with each step.

Felicia and I exchanged a momentary glance before bolting after him. We couldn't let him go on alone, after all. The train was still lumbering past us, but as we ran, it seemed to slow down. I know now that it wasn't really slowing, we were just starting to equal its pace. The boxcars were still rolling on ahead, but they were no longer passing at such an impossible speed. Finally, the last car of the train clamored up alongside us and Samuel gathered enough courage to jump for it.

I'm not sure how he did it, but his entire body launched through the air like an arrow, giving him just enough distance and height to latch his fingers around the metal railing and drag himself into the wide, gaping door of the boxcar.

Once inside, he stuck his head and shoulders back out the door and waved to us. "Hurry!" he screamed, his voice barely sounding over the train.

To our great fortune, the iron beast had come to a slight curve in the track up ahead, which forced it to reduce its speed a bit. Felicia and I knew this was our chance. Our legs were already tired and burning from the journey through the forest, but we had no choice. We had to give it all we had.

Felicia was first. With her teeth gritted tightly, she managed to gain on the final boxcar and leap up with her hand outstretched. To his credit, Samuel managed to catch her by the arm on the first try and somehow hold her there, making sure she didn't fall. With her free hand, Felicia tried to help pull herself inside by grabbing the frame of the door, only to lose her grip on the paper pamphlet that Pa had given her.

"No!" Felicia shrieked. I was barely even aware of the pamphlet as it fluttered by my head and became lost in the windy wake of the train.

"Forget it!" Samuel told her. "It's gone! Now, come on!"

With a strained heave, Samuel dragged Felicia into the car and helped her to her feet. A few seconds later, they were both waving for me to get to them.

It was my turn, now. Lowering my head, I pumped my arms as hard as I could manage, and I pushed my legs as fast as they could go. I was known for my speed, but now it was time to live up to it. The train had mostly passed the curve and was beginning to speed up once more. This was my only chance. It was now or never.

I was positively sucking wind into my lungs as I ran. Felicia and Samuel both crouched down to the floor of the boxcar, reaching their hands out to get as close to me as they could. I was nearly there. The gravel under my feet was giving me quite a challenge, but it wasn't going to stop me. I was so close. I knew I could make it if I jumped. As I stuck my arm up to grab a helping hand, my balance tipped too far forward and I lost my footing.

The entire world fell into slow motion. The train sounds disappeared entirely, and my sister's horrified scream was completely muted as my body floated toward the ground.

WHAM!

I hit with a terrible force, feeling the sharp edges of the gravel gnashing at my clothes and exposed flesh. The air exploded from my lungs in one huge gust as I slid forward on my stomach. Trying my best to ignore the pain, I put my hands underneath me and lifted my head, only to see the train receding into the distance. They were too far away now. I would never catch them. Unbelievable fear was all I could feel in that moment. I had lost my brother and sister. They were now headed to freedom and I was stuck here in the middle of nowhere by myself . . . lost. A terrible despair engulfed me and I could only wail mournfully into the humid night air.

Chapter 4

Suddenly, there were hands underneath me, powerful, calloused hands that scooped me off the ground in one fluid motion. In front of my eyes, Felicia and Samuel were now growing, coming closer rather than drifting away. Above me, I heard the labored breathing of my father as he flew like the wind, carrying me in his arms like I weighed nothing at all. I couldn't even speak. Pa had come for me. He had come to my rescue and was doing everything in his power to make sure I could get away from life on the plantation. I believe it was in that moment that I began to understand the sacrifice he was making.

Pa ran like a thoroughbred alongside that train. In just a few seconds, he had caught up to the last car as it was rounding the curve. With one final grunt of effort, Pa dove forward, shoving me right into the waiting arms of Samuel and Felicia. They both seized ahold of me tightly and all three of us tumbled backward into the empty boxcar. As soon as I found my wits, I scrambled off of them and stuck my head out the boxcar door, letting the wind ruffle my bushy hair as it rushed past me.

In the distance, I saw Pa rolling on the ground for just a moment before standing up and looking in my direction. Still in disbelief, I stuck an arm out to wave at him and let him know I had made it. In truth, it felt a lot like I was really waving goodbye. In the distance, I saw him raise his arm above his head and give his own parting wave, a gesture that sent more hot tears cascading down my flushed cheeks. A few seconds later, the slender silhouette of Ma came trotting down to stand beside him and they both stood in the night's shadow, watching us disappear. We had no choice but to do the same.

When they had completely faded from view, none of us could find any words that seemed fit to speak. Slowly, we slumped down to the floor of the car, all of us hunkered together on our knees, our minds racing with uncertainty. What were we going to do now? Where was this train going on the way to Reading? Would we be caught? How would we hide? What were we going to eat? It took several long minutes before the silence between us was broken.

"We're gonna be all right," Felicia said. I couldn't help but notice that her eyes were fixed on the wood-plank floor beneath us.

"Are we?" I asked timidly.

Felicia nodded, but still couldn't lift her gaze. "Don't worry. Neither of you."

"What about Ma and Pa?" Samuel asked from beside me.

Once again, the three of us fell silent, our thoughts wandering back to our parents, still standing by the dark, silent railroad tracks, listening to a train carry away their only children into the night. All I could do was stare out the gaping door of the train car, watching the countryside whip by in the pale moonlight. My knees and abdomen still ached from the fall I had taken, and my hands were still burning from the gravel wounds, but I could think of nothing except my mother and father. It was hard to believe that we had been sleeping comfortably in our cabin just a few hours earlier.

As my thoughts drifted to the cabin, I couldn't help but wonder what Mr. Slate would do, what Tomstin himself would do, once they discovered that all of us were gone. All the Dawson kids missing at once? The morning count would be three short and Tomstin would surely go straight to Ma and Pa. What would they say? That we all ran away? At the same time? My mind began to fill with the horrible thought of their punishment. What would they have to endure for trying to free us? The whip? The club? Something worse?

The notion that I might never see them again overtook me, and I began to weep silently. Rather than seek comfort from my siblings, I simply retreated into the boxcar and huddled in the corner, holding my head in my hands.

My mother and father were the best people I had ever known. I was sure they were going to be killed, I just knew it. I began to feel grief as if they had already died. I think my ten-year-old mind could only think of it that way, like they were already gone. I had spent every single day of my life with them. To suddenly be cast into the world without the security that they gave me . . . it truly felt as if they were gone for good.

It broke my heart.

After I spent a solitary minute sobbing in the corner, Felicia crawled over to where I was and leaned herself against me, wrapping her arm around my shoulders. A part of me wanted to tell her to get away, to stop touching me and stop pretending it was all right. I wanted to believe it was her fault. I wanted to believe . . . maybe . . . that if she had just refused Pa's orders, we would all still be together. The three of us wouldn't be stuck on this miserable, stinking train going somewhere new and terrifying while half our family was gone forever.

It was a foolish thought, I know. Besides, I couldn't be mad at her. She and Samuel were all

I had left now. As Samuel scuttled over to sit by us, I knew that they were both thinking the same thing that I was: we needed each other.

If we were going to survive out in the world, we would have to stay together. Alone, there was no way that any of us would make it. Together, we had a chance. As the train chugged its way through the night, I said a silent goodbye to my mother and father, telling them that I loved them and I wished they would be safe.

I could only hope that they heard me.

*** *** ***

Jefferson Tomstin rubbed his weary eyes as the carriage rattled loudly down the dirt path to the fields. He groaned quietly as he jostled back and forth on the padded bench seat, wondering just why he had been summoned. "Mr. Slate says there's a problem with the kids," the messenger had said. Tomstin had grudgingly slipped into his trousers and boots and rousted his driver. Whatever the problem was, it had better be something important.

Tomstin turned his head to the right and gazed curiously down at his son, Georgeo, who was rocking and jostling right next to him. Tomstin watched him from his peripheral vision, wondering why he had volunteered to come. He had never before expressed an interest in dealing with the field workers. What was so different about this particular morning? Tomstin had a hunch, but if it was correct, Georgeo was more suspect than he seemed.

As the carriage finally rounded the last bend, the slave cabins came into view, and Tomstin leaned to the left, sticking his head out the window to see if he could determine the problem from a distance. As the wagon got closer, he could see the entire slave population standing together in a semi-circle, surrounding Sam and Mr. Slate. He also saw two of the workers manacled to a whipping post. Instantaneously, Tomstin's weariness was gone, replaced by seething aggravation. When the messenger had said there was a problem with the children, Tomstin had assumed one of them had fallen ill or had broken a limb. Something simple. Something manageable. As the carriage rolled to a stop, he could tell things were not going to be as such. As it happened, he was quite familiar with the couple who were now tied to the post. He knew of them and their children. With one final suspicious glance back at Georgeo, Tomstin stepped out of the carriage and slipped his leather suspender straps over his shoulders.

"What is all this?" he asked as he stomped toward his Slave Master.

Slate drew a deep breath and nodded to the couple on the post. "All three kids are missing as of this morning. Nowhere to be found."

Tomstin felt his lips pulling back over his teeth, tightening as the blood began to simmer in his veins. "Well, where are they?"

Slate spotted Blue, Nate, and Elijah standing in front of a cabin. Wasting no time, he marched over to them and barked, "I want to know right now! He must have told you something! Where are they?"

He continued to glare at the men while waiting for an answer but the men just stood frozen in fear. "Speak now or I swear to you, there will be blood! Come on, speak!" yelled out Slate. "Duke never told me nothin'," uttered Blue. "Not a word, Master Slate, not a word."

Slate turned and let out a grunt in disgust. Then he walked over to Tomstin. "He's lying and the rest of them ain't talkin'," he said. "But, I did find this on 'em." From the pocket of his slacks, he drew a tattered, filthy scrap of paper and held it out for Tomstin to see. When he bent down, squinting hard to decipher the words and diagrams through the dirt, Tomstin's anger boiled over.

"A train?" he spat, looking toward Duke and Elizabeth. "You put 'em on a train, didn't you?"

The father, Duke, simply blinked his eyes, staring right past Tomstin and into the distance. His attempt at remaining stoic was only serving to further agitate Tomstin.

"Where's that train go?" he asked furiously.

Slate shook his head. "I ain't sure. But, I do know that they could be hundreds of miles from here by now. They also could have jumped off at any point during the trip. Sorry to say, but they could be anywhere, sir."

With an enraged growl, Tomstin grasped the paper in his hand and quickly crushed it into a ball before throwing it away in disgust. With all eyes now on him, he turned away from Slate, repeatedly running his fingers through his hair as he paced angrily across the dirt. After a moment, he turned his fiery gaze upon Duke.

"You!" he snarled. In a split second, he had stomped over to where Duke stood tied and was stang up at him, trying to keep his breathing steady. "You thought you were clever, huh? You thought you could slip away one night and remove property that belongs to *me*!" He couldn't help but shout the last word, watching as Duke's face barely flinched.

"How long were ya plannin' it, boy?" Tomstin asked, spraying flecks of saliva from between his yellowed teeth. "How long were you plannin' to stab me in the back? *Tell me!*"

The massive group of workers stirred uncomfortably at Tomstin's rage, but Slate's squad of armed gunhands kept them at bay. They had seen Tomstin angry before, but this was something else entirely. They had never seen this. In his frenzied state, he enjoyed seeing the fear in their eyes. He enjoyed the timid way that they shifted their weight back and forth on their feet. They feared him. That was the way he preferred it. After all, fear meant obedience. He knew that as long as they were afraid of what he could do to them, they would remain under his power. The two miscreants tied to the post, however, did not fear him enough. He was going to correct that.

"Well!" Tomstin shouted, turning to address the large audience before him. "These events have undoubtedly been planned and prepared for by these two," he gestured to Duke and Elizabeth, "and they were surely resigned to paying dearly for their act of betrayal."

The slaves made not one sound. The whole lot of them had given Tomstin their undivided attention. He knew he had to use it to send a message.

He gave one last sinister smile in Duke's direction and then turned to Slate, nodding his head in the couple's direction. "Cut 'em loose."

Slate's heavy brow wrinkled slightly at the words. "Sir?"

"They knew this was coming," Tomstin explained. "They were prepared to be punished. I'm gonna give 'em something they *weren't* prepared for. Now, cut them loose."

Slate's lips twisted into a slight grimace, but he did as he was ordered. Taking slow steps, he made his way to Duke and Elizabeth and swiftly untied the leather straps that had held them in place. Their arms fell to their sides, but neither of them made any attempt to move.

Once he knew they were watching him, Tomstin marched over to the crowd of workers who were serving as his audience. His eyes were locked on a small boy near the front. "You," Tomstin said, pointing his bony finger at the youngster. "What's your name?"

The boy looked up at him for several long seconds before finally muttering "Munroe, sir."

"Munroe," Tomstin repeated, nodding his head. "Yes, you'll do just fine."

In a swift motion, Tomstin reached out and seized the young boy's hand, yanking him away from his father. He muscled past his fellow workers as Tomstin dragged his son toward the whipping post.

"No, wait! You can't—" The butt of a rifle across his temple was enough to cut the father's sentence short. As he crumpled to the ground, his woman rushed forward to kneel beside him.

"Master Tomstin, please!" she begged. "Don't hurt Munroe. He's done nothin' wrong!" She draped her body protectively over her mate as she pleaded for her son's safety. Had it been any other day, Tomstin would have been amused by such a showing. Today, however, it only angered him further.

"Shut up!" he roared at her. Jerking the boy by the arm, Tomstin thrust the child toward Slate. "Give me the whip and tie up this boy."

Wordlessly, Slate obeyed, handing over the whip before leading the bewildered-looking boy to the post. Behind him, Tomstin gestured to the nearest gunhand, directing him to shuffle Munroe's parents back into the crowd where they came from. Despite the concern for their child, they had no choice but to comply. They knew Tomstin wouldn't hesitate to let bullets fly if it came to it, and he was glad they knew it.

As Slate finished binding Munroe's hands above his head, he lifted the boy's shirt over his head, exposing the dark skin of his back. The youngster already bore the scars of a few run-ins with a hickory switch, but they would be nothing compared to those of a full-sized bullwhip. Once all was in place, Tomstin turned again to address the uneasy crowd before him.

"I am not the enemy here!" Tomstin shouted. "I have been nothing but kind to you people. Do I not feed you? The food that you eat, the water that you drink, does it not come from me? Is it not paid for out of my own pocket? Do I not give every last one of you a place to live, a place to lay your heads at night?" He began slowly pacing up and down the line of slaves, glaring intently at them until they broke their gaze and looked away in fear. "I hear so many you whisper about freedom. Freedom! Here, I give you something more! I give you something more than freedom!" He paused for several moments before adding "I give you *purpose!*"

Tomstin allowed the thought to linger on their minds. He allowed it to soak into their very skin. Every facet of their lives was controlled by him. He controlled how much they ate or drank or slept. He controlled when and where they could urinate. Most importantly of all, he controlled whether they lived or died. On his land, he was their god, and it was high time they truly began to respect him as such.

"One of your own is responsible for this!" Tomstin went on. "Not I. It was one of your own who perpetrated these events. I am sorry to say that my lenience has been taken advantage of and the axe must fall on someone." He pointed to Munroe, still strapped tightly to the post, trembling. "This boy's fate is not in my hands. My hands are being forced! I am being made to do this! Because of them!" He moved his finger slightly to the left, centering it on Duke and Elizabeth.

Tomstin gave them a fiery glare before turning back to his captive audience. "Those two have put me in a position that I am not accustomed to nor enjoy. But as the proprietor of this great land, it is my duty to ensure that something like this doesn't ever . . . *ever* . . . happen again!"

With a dramatic sigh, he turned to look at Munroe, who now had silent tears rolling down his sunken cheeks. "It saddens me," Tomstin said, "to think that a child must now bear the scars of this betrayal. After all I do for each of you, this is how I am treated? With contempt? Well, it seems I have been too kind to you all. I have been too patient. Let it be known . . . that ends today! Despite the kindness I have shown all of you, you see me as the enemy? If that's so, then perhaps that is who I need to be. This child will bear the scars to remind all of you that I am never to be crossed!"

The crowd was deathly silent. The only sounds were the muted sobs of Munroe's mother as she lamented her son's regrettable fate. "Please, Master Tomstin!" she cried. "Please, don't! Munroe is innocent, sir. He's . . . he's a real fine boy, Master, I beg you. Please, find it in your heart not to do this!"

Tomstin simply shook his head at her words. "As I said before, my hands are being forced. Mr. Slate."

Tomstin didn't even have to give an order. Immediately, Slate drew the shining silver revolver from his hip and leveled it at the hysterical mother, causing her to effectively lock her lips. Large tears continued to stream heavily from her brown eyes, but she wisely said nothing more.

"My kindness has been mistaken for weakness!" Tomstin shouted. "And it ends now." With a swift, experienced motion, Tomstin unfurled the whip and squared himself toward Munroe, who was now squirming nervously against the wooden post. Raising his arm, Tomstin tightened his fist around the whip handle. "It ends *now*!"

"Stop!" screamed a voice from the road.

Distracted, Tomstin paused with his arm in the air. "What in the . . . ?"

Before Tomstin could move another muscle, Georgeo had reached his side and had seized a hold of his elbow.

"Don't do it!" Georgeo said loudly, staring intently up at his father.

Tomstin looked down at him, his face marred with shock and anger. "Boy . . . what do you think you are doing?"

"Stop this, please!" Georgeo replied.

"Let *me* go, boy!" Tomstin snapped back, jerking his arm out of his son's grasp. In response, Georgeo bent down and scooped the end of the whip out of the dirt, wrapping both of his hands around it to prevent it from being used.

Tomstin's face burned red hot. He could feel every eye of every slave staring intently at him, watching as his own son, nothing more than a child, stood against him. He wasn't about to let some bratty whelp undermine the fear and respect for him that he had conditioned his workers to keep—even if that whelp was his own blood.

"You drop that whip," Tomstin growled furiously through gritted teeth. "Right . . . now!"

"Please," Georgeo said, attempting to appeal to Tomstin's better nature. "Please, Father. You shouldn't do this."

"You are embarrassing yourself!" Tomstin snarled. "Let go of the whip! Now!"

Georgeo shook his head defiantly. "Not until you stop this!"

Tomstin's rage had hit its peak. With a loud grunt, he drew back his free hand and swung it hard at Georgeo's face, listening with satisfaction as the slap resounded loudly across the field. With a grunt of shock and pain, Georgeo fell back from the force of the blow, landing hard in the dirt by his father's feet. His spectacles skittered to a stop a few yards behind where he lay.

With his teeth bared in fury, Tomstin bent down to Georgeo's ear. "Perhaps you're right," he said in a hushed tone. "Perhaps it *shouldn't* be me doing this. I do believe it should be you."

Georgeo's head snapped up at these words, revealing the red welt underneath his left eye. He gave no reply, but his face was contracted into an expression of pure disdain, one that Tomstin hadn't quite expected to see.

"I've heard some things," Tomstin went on, making no attempt to hide the accusation in his voice. "For some time, now . . . I've been hearing that you and one of them runaways, one of the boys, are friends."

The rush of blood to Georgeo's neck and ears was all the confirmation Tomstin needed. He smiled at the sight.

"Yeah, you and him are pals," Tomstin said, still bearing his wry grin. "Aren't ya?"

Still remaining silent, Georgeo slowly got to his feet, keeping his eyes locked on Tomstin's as he dusted off his tan slacks. He continued to stare daggers at his father, as if he were trying to make the man spontaneously combust with his mind.

"Answer me!" Tomstin bellowed. The look of protest on his son's face was disconcerting. He liked it better when the boy would just cower and obey. He needed Georgeo to learn the same thing that all these slaves were learning today: Jefferson Tomstin is not to be crossed!

"Now would be a good time for you to be truthful," Tomstin said gravely.

Georgeo continued to stare at him for several more seconds before finally parting his lips to speak. "Yes."

Tomstin held his hand to his ear. "I couldn't hear that. What was that you said?"

"Yes!" Georgeo shouted. His face was turning an even darker shade of red. "He is my friend."

Tomstin nodded. Despite the fact that he'd had his suspicions, the answer was no less jarring to hear. He wondered if Georgeo had known beforehand that those slaves were going to disappear. He would get to the bottom of that later. Right now, there was still a lesson to be taught.

"So, you *are* friends . . . with a slave," Tomstin said, feeling the words burn like acid on his tongue. "Well, just how good of a friend is he?"

"Best friend!" Georgeo exclaimed, his voice bold and challenging.

Tomstin drew a deep breath and let it out in a huff. His disgust was evident in his scowl. "That's just fantastic," he drawled. "See, where I come from, a man would do just about anything to help a friend: lend him some tools, money, help him build a house, help him break a horse, anything."

Georgeo remained silent, wondering where his father was going with his train of thought.

"I'm gonna give you a chance, boy," Tomstin continued. "I'm gonna give you a chance right now, in front of me, in front of this community here, in front of God himself, to prove just how much this . . . *friend* . . . of yours means to you."

Georgeo's only reply was his scathing glare.

Tomstin grinned at him. "You're gonna need that fire, boy. I got a deal for you." He knelt down next to his son, holding the whip out to him as if he were presenting a gift. "Take this," Tomstin murmured. "You administer three sound lashes—three lashes from you instead of ten from me—and I will make no attempt in retrieving my lost workers. How's that sound?"

Georgeo's expression changed immediately. His hardened glower transformed into a look of disbelief. He took a step back from his father, a step away from the whip that was being offered.

Tomstin shook his head. "Bear in mind . . . that if you refuse, I will dedicate every resource I can muster, I will find those three runaways, including your so-called best friend, and I will put them in the ground! All of them!"

The anger began to return to Georgeo's eyes as they darted back and forth from Tomstin to the whip. With a seemingly great effort, he slowly raised a trembling hand, reaching forth and taking the handle of the whip in his fingers.

"That's it," Tomstin said with a devious smile. "Believe me when I say that you're making the right decision, son." As he rose to his feet, he stepped to the side, creating a clear line of sight to Munroe, who still stood tied to the wooden post by the road.

"Three lashes!" Tomstin called out. "No more, no less!"

Georgeo stepped forward nervously, stepping lightly from side to side. His eyes were wide and terrified, but he raised his arm, ready to crack the leather whip in his hand.

"Go on," Tomstin urged.

Georgeo brought his arm down and took several deep breaths before raising it again . . . and then dropping it once more. With his breathing becoming shallow, he raised his arm for a third time, holding it in the air for several moments before letting it drop.

"I can't," he said, defeated.

Clicking his tongue, Tomstin stepped forward and bent down to address him. "Some friend you are," he said, rubbing salt in the wound. "I guess it's up to me, isn't it?"

Georgeo shut his eyes tight as he tried to keep his lip from quivering. Without a word, he held out the weapon for his father to take.

"I'm quite handy with a whip," Tomstin said to him. "Ten lashes from me might just kill him. That would make four deaths to be weighing on your shoulders tonight."

"No!" Georgeo wailed. He shoved hard against his father's shoulder, moving him away. "You want three lashes? Fine!"

Without wasting another moment on contemplation, Georgeo raised his arm and jerked it to the side, bringing the narrow end of the leather right across Munroe's exposed back.

CRACK!
CRACK!
CRACK!

Georgeo finished the three lashes in quick succession, doing all he could to minimize the torment. Munroe's cries of anguish, however, were still echoing across the vast fields, ringing loudly in the ears of everyone present.

Georgeo could only cover his face in shame as his shoulders silently heaved in the morning sun. "I'm sorry," he finally croaked out. He turned his head to glance toward Munroe's parents, his tears matching those on their faces. "I'm sorry!"

His words did little to ease them.

"I knew you had it in you, boy!" Tomstin said boisterously, clapping a heavy hand on Georgeo's shoulder. "I'm proud of you. Truly." Still smiling, he glanced around at the crowd before him. "Look at 'em, son," he said. "Look at their faces."

Slowly, Georgeo turned his head to peer out at them, still crying silent tears as the workers looked at him in surprise.

"They fear you now," Tomstin said, nodding with satisfaction. "With fear comes respect."

In a sudden flash of anger, Georgeo shrugged off his father's hand and threw the whip into the dirt with a loud grunt. "I want your word!" he shouted, rounding on Tomstin. "I want your word that no one else will be hurt!"

Taken aback by the sudden outburst, Tomstin could only nod, holding his hands up in a move of mock surrender. "You have my word," he said genuinely. "Cut him loose!"

Slate, who had remained silent and motionless since tying Munroe to the post, finally moved once more to free the boy. At once, Munroe collapsed to the dry ground and his parents rushed forward to help him to his feet.

"It's gonna be all right," his mother said soothingly as she stroked his cheek. "You'll be better in no time."

Unwilling to watch the fallout of his actions, Georgeo gave the whip a final kick before storming back to the carriage.

Tomstin let him go. As he bent down to retrieve the whip, he motioned for Slate to join him.

"Yes, sir?" Slate asked, stepping over to his employer.

"I want you to take two men," Tomstin said quietly. "Two of your best. You take them to hunt down and find those runaways. I don't care what it costs, you understand?"

"I do, sir," Slate responded stiffly. "And when they find them?"

Tomstin drew a slow breath before answering. "Bullets are cheap. Don't be stingy with them."

As he turned and strolled back to the carriage, Slate gave a simple nod. "Yes, sir."

Chapter 5

The shrill, piercing sound of a steam whistle was enough to pull me out of my deep sleep. I didn't open my eyes, not even when I felt Felicia rousing beside me. As I felt the gentle rocking motion of the train beneath me, I suddenly remembered where I was. I was no longer on the plantation. For the first time in my entire life, I was waking up somewhere else, somewhere unfamiliar, somewhere other than that one-room cabin next to the cotton field. I wanted to go back to sleep. I was safe there. I was somewhere comfortable and not abandoned in a boxcar. Maybe if I squinted my eyes hard enough, I could go back into a dream where I was with my mother and father.

After a moment, Felicia got to her feet and moved toward the door of the car. Shortly after that, Samuel sluggishly stood up and followed her, leaving me alone on the floor of the train car. Without them around me, the rushing wind felt much colder. Despite my shivering skin, I still believed I could make it back to sleep if I tried. I wrapped my arms tightly around my mid-section and curled into a ball. Faintly, I heard Samuel open his mouth and speak.

"Is this . . . free? Are we free?" he asked.

Felicia was silent for a few seconds before replying. "I think so," she said optimistically. In my morning grogginess, I couldn't help but feel a tiny bit of relief at her words. If she was right, then we wouldn't have to worry about evading capture anymore. We would only have to worry about finding food and shelter.

Suddenly, there was a terrible crashing that sounded from the opposite corner of the boxcar. The noise was enough to remove any hope I had of getting back to sleep. With my eyes now wide open, I scrambled to my feet and backed against the wall, wondering just what it was that I had heard. By the door, Felicia and Samuel were both wearing the same startled expression that I was. It took only a moment to discover that the clattering had come from an empty wooden crate that had tumbled to the floor. The opposite corner held several of these crates, and from behind them, a strange moaning could be heard.

After taking a moment to look at one another, Felicia and Samuel edged closer to the crates, investigating the sounds. I couldn't deny my own curiosity as I followed just behind them. Together, the three of us peeked over the wooden boxes and were slightly surprised to discover that we hadn't been alone as we slept. The thought was a little disturbing, but as we looked down at this man that was slowly regaining consciousness, we could tell he wasn't going to give us any trouble.

The thing that struck me first was the smell. He stank like a field worker who hadn't had a bath in weeks. There was something else, though, something familiar. As the man lifted a filthy hand to rub his equally filthy face, an empty brown, glass bottle rolled away from him. I knew what the smell was. It was the same thing Master Tomstin would smell like some afternoons when he'd wander down to the fields. I wasn't sure what exactly the drink was, but I knew it made him meaner and more cruel than usual. Louder, too. If this stranger was drinking the same thing, he might just be a handful.

The odor wasn't the only thing off about him. His skin looked as though it had once been white. Now, though, it was covered in a layer of dirt and grime so thick that he appeared mostly grey in color. His hair was mostly grey, streaked with a few sections that were still dark, and it was so greasy and stringy that it looked wet. His beard was thick and full of dirt, but it wasn't that long. He must have had a shave a few weeks ago. Why he hadn't cut his hair was beyond me. What kind of life was this fellow leading?

Before any of us could find something to say, the man slowly opened his bleary, bloodshot eyes. He blinked several times, trying to get them to open and close in unison. Upon seeing the three of us looking down at him, the man only groaned again and slowly rolled onto his side, coughing loudly.

"You all right, Mister?" Felicia asked.

In response, the man held up a hand to stop her. "Shhh!" he hissed. "Quit yellin'." It was then that I noticed that his left hand was missing its pinky finger. I immediately wanted to know how he had lost it, but I knew it wasn't the best time to ask.

"Who are you?" Felicia queried.

"Shhh," the man responded again.

Felicia looked over at Samuel and me before asking once more, this time keeping her voice noticeably softer. "Who are you?"

With a pained groan, the man rolled over to his stomach before slowly pushing himself up to his knees. After taking a few deep breaths, the man looked over at Felicia, squinting against the bright light of the morning. "The name's Seth," he answered. "Who might you be, if I may ask?"

"Well, my name is—"

"Shhh . . ."

Felicia rolled her eyes. "My name is Felicia," she said in a hushed tone. "This here's my brother Samuel, and that's my little brother Isaac."

"Peachy," Seth said, wincing noticeably as he stretched his back.

"Are you all right?" I asked him.

Seth looked over at me, his eyebrows pulling together as he sighed. "If I was all right, you think I'd be on this here train?"

I didn't answer him.

"You ain't got something to drink, do ya?" He asked, sounding like he already knew the answer. "Something stiff? Something with a good kick?"

Together, the three of us shook our heads.

"That's not something you need, anyhow," I said, kicking the empty bottle that he had been sleeping with.

Seth gave a short, raspy laugh. "Well . . . thanks for the advice, kid. Now, here's you some: Don't ever drink with a big woman," he gingerly climbed to his feet, breathing hard like it was taking a monumental effort. "You'll wake up one morning with her screaming at you, the house is full of kids who are screaming at you, and you'll have a big, nasty hangover that lasts for six years."

"I'll . . . keep that in mind," I said, totally clueless as to what he was talking about.

Seth nodded, wagging a bony finger at me. "You do that."

He leaned over onto the crates that had hidden him during the night, peering out the wide boxcar door. He drew in a deep breath through his nose and then sighed with disappointment.

"Welp!" he said, scratching his matted hair. "I'm gonna lay back down. Do me a favor and wake me at the next stop, would ya?"

Seth looked behind him at the spot where he had spent the last several hours. He began to sink toward the ground, like laying down was going to be as difficult as standing up.

"Pardon me, Mister . . . uh . . . Seth," Felicia stammered. "Where *is* the next stop?"

Seth stood straight again and looked up at her. "That would be Alexandria, Missy."

Felicia toyed nervously with her fingernails. "Is that anywhere near Reading?"

"Reading" Seth asked, staring hard at her.

"Reading, Pennsylvania," she clarified.

For a long moment, Seth just stared at her, his left eyebrow cocked in confusion. "No." he finally said. "No, no . . . this train hasn't gone North in some time. They changed the route a few years back. Didn't you know that?"

At once, all three of us exchanged terrified glances. The train must have switched tracks while we were sleeping and it doesn't take a genius to know this was bad. After all, we had left everything we knew to get on a train that we had thought was going North to freedom. In reality, we had been going in the opposite direction all along. What on earth were we going to do now? How could we fix this?

Felicia swallowed hard, her eyes still wide with shock. "No, we didn't know that."

"So, you're saying this train is actually running South instead of North?" I asked, hoping he would let out another laugh and say he had only been joking.

To my dismay, Seth nodded. "That's right. There's only one train that goes North now. That's the Oh-Nine."

Samuel rubbed his bald head, his gaze fixed somewhere in the distance. "What are we gonna do?"

"We need to get on that train," Felicia said urgently.

Samuel scoffed at her. "How we gonna do that?"

Before anyone could answer, Seth shoved hard against one of the crates in front of him, knocking it out of his way as he made for the door. I was surprised at how strong he was, especially considering his current physical state. Curiously, the three of us followed after him, making our way to the open side of the boxcar. Despite our suddenly dire predicament, I couldn't help but admire the incredible scenery that was gliding by in front of me.

There were mountains. Up until that point in my life, I had never before laid eyes on a mountain. They were so tall, silhouetted purplish against the grey morning sky. I wondered what it would be like to climb them, to stand on the very top and yell out across the world. In front of those mountains, a wonderful set of rolling hills and golden valleys shone vibrantly in the early sunlight. It was quite a sight, something I had never laid eyes on. Maybe it wasn't quite freedom, but it sure looked like it. Especially compared to a cotton field.

"You're in luck," Seth said, snapping me out of my trance. "You see that mountain there?"

Felicia nodded, staring into the distance, surely dumbfounded by the same sight that captured me.

"All right," Seth went on. "On the other side of that mountain, you'll find the little town of Chesterfield. The train you need, the Oh-Nine, it pulls in there once a week. From here, it ought to take you five . . . maybe six days to get there. If you hurry, though, you can make it there by the time that train pulls out."

Felicia nodded again, listening intently to Seth's instructions.

"It ain't gonna be easy, mind you," Seth said gravely, gesturing to the hills and valleys. "It's a hard way to go . . . especially for a group of escaped slaves."

Samuel and I looked at each other, panic lighting up our eyes again. I suppose our general clueless nature was a dead giveaway, but I still hadn't expected a disheveled hobo to be able to pick up on it so quickly.

Noticing the fear frozen on all of our faces, Seth gave a raspy chuckle. "Yeah, I figured as much." He leaned down next to Felicia and put his hand on her shoulder. "You'll have to watch yourself. There's plenty of slave patrols between here and Chesterfield."

I chanced a glance out the boxcar door, feeling the cool wind stinging my eyes. I didn't see Alexandria, the town that Seth had said was the next stop, but I wondered if there was a clear road from there to Chesterfield.

"So," I said to him, "When the train stops, we can—"

"Oh, you can't wait that long," Seth said, scratching his hairy, sallow cheek. "By the time this train stops, that mountain and that town are gonna be long gone. If you're gonna make it there and ride that rail north to Reading, you're gonna have to jump. Right now."

I blinked up at him. "Jump?"

"You'd better make it fast!" Seth prodded. The urgency was clear in his voice. "The longer you wait, the further away Chesterfield gets! What's it gonna be?"

Once more, I felt panic begin to rise in my throat. I stared out at the mountain in the distance, watching as it slowly slid along the horizon. Was that really where we needed to go? I had been fantasizing just a moment before about climbing that mountain, and now that I had discovered our path intended for me to do just that, I was more than a little intimidated by the thought.

"We have to jump," Felicia said matter-of-factly.

I know Samuel would have loved to argue with her, but there would have been no use. He knew she was right, same as I did. "You first," he said to her.

Felicia nodded. With her jaw quivering, she exhaled slowly and stepped up to the door, staring down at the ground.

"Remember!" Seth shouted, trying to make himself heard over the roaring wind. "When you hit, don't try and land upright! You'll just end up falling over. Hit with your feet first, then tuck into a ball and roll with it! Trust me!"

Felicia gulped loudly. "Okay!"

"You ready?" Seth asked.

She nodded.

He put his hand on the center of her back and gave a hefty shove. "Jump!"

Felicia had no choice. She vanished from sight with a choked cry of surprise. Isaac and I didn't even have time to look out the door after her before Seth was grabbing both of us by the scruffs of our necks.

"Y'all are next!"

Without a word, Samuel grasped my hand in his and leapt out of the moving train, dragging me along behind him.

Once again, the world fell into slow motion. Even so, the tall, swaying grass was still zipping by underneath me at an alarming rate. For a moment, it felt like I was just hovering over it, flying along like some kind of magician. The very next instant, I was crashing down into it, gritting my teeth and squeezing my eyes shut as

I tried to follow Seth's "tuck-and-roll" tutorial. Thankfully, the thick grass made a much better cushion than the gravel had last night. As Samuel and I finally rolled to a stop, we simply looked at one another, our eyes wide with adrenaline, and then burst into laughter.

After a few seconds, Felicia dashed over to where we lay in the grass. She could tell by our relieved giggling that we were unhurt. She let out a sigh of relief and bent down to Samuel, hoisting him to his feet so he could do the same for me.

"Thanks, Seth!" she called loudly, waving to the train.

As I turned around, I saw the steel beast growing smaller in the distance. From the last boxcar, a small figure waved back to us as the engine's black smoke billowed into the warming air. "Good thing he was around," I said, watching the train disappear.

Felicia nodded. "Sure enough. We'd best get moving, though, like he said."

Without questioning her, Samuel and I fell in beside her and we took our first steps toward the mountain that Seth had specified. We were hungry, thirsty, and not exactly in the mood for a cross-country trek, but we all knew there was no choice. We had to make it to Chesterfield and board that train to Reading. Together, the three of us set off into the wilderness, not knowing anything of the journey that lay before us.

The tall grass made progress slow, but it wasn't so terrible. Even as the sun rose higher in the sky, the heat seemed less severe and not as hot on our shoulders as it had been back in the fields. The thing that was most difficult to handle were the mosquitoes. I didn't know why, but those hills were swarming with them. The three of us sounded like an amateur drum corps as we went, slapping and beating on ourselves every time we felt one of the little monsters bite.

Though we weren't exactly free at the moment, I had never felt more freedom in my life. For the first time since we'd all been born, no one had awakened us on a schedule. No one had hurried us through a lukewarm breakfast. No one had counted us or ordered us into a cotton field. We'd never experienced anything like it. We were on our own schedule. If we wanted to drop to the ground and take a nap, we could. No one could tell us different.

The only downside was the rumble in our bellies and the scratchiness in the backs of our throats. The sun was starting to hang low in the blue sky and we hadn't had anything to eat or drink all day. None of us complained about it. Mostly because we knew there was nothing that could be done, but also because we had been conditioned to keep our lips together during the day. As we hiked further and further across the landscape, we got slower and slower, worn down by the sun, the humid air, and the energy it took to wade through the primordial growth of grass and weeds. By the time we finally heard the distant rush of river water, it sounded as wonderful as a chorus of heaven's angels.

"Up here!" Samuel shouted, fighting his way through the waist-high grass. "It's a river, sure enough!"

Felicia and I scurried behind him, desperate to finally soothe our dry, aching throats. "Oh, thank goodness," Felicia breathed.

There it was: the river, in all its glory!

The river was quite wide where we were, and the water was moving at a good speed. Stray leaves and blades of grass could be seen floating on the surface, surging along between rocks and along the banks. The water itself was a beautiful pale blue. If it had been still, there was no doubt I could have seen right to the bottom. As it was, with the surface all frothy, there was no way to tell just how deep it was. Fortunately, no matter how fast the water was moving, it was still drinkable.

Simultaneously, the three of us dropped to our knees at the river's edge and began scooping handfuls of the fresh, ice-cold water to our mouths. After a moment, we all gave up and resorted to sticking our entire faces beneath the surface to drink faster. As I came up for breath, the cold water dripping down my neck and chest was an incredible relief. It felt so good on my sun-scorched flesh that I dipped my hand back into the water and splashed some of it onto myself, gasping at how icy it was. Instantly, the cotton in our mouths was gone. Our bellies, while still in need of food, were filled to the brim with delicious water that was cooling us down from the inside out.

For a while, the three of us relaxed there on the riverbank, breathing deeply and relishing the feeling of being momentarily satisfied. For a long time, we didn't speak. There didn't seem to be anything important enough to say. But, as the sun began to get lower and lower, Felicia finally opened her mouth to break the silence.

"We're gonna have to cross, you know," she said. Her tone sounded almost apologetic, like she was sorry for breaking the mood. It didn't make her words any less heavy, though. Samuel and I knew she was right.

At that moment, we rose to our feet. As we stood up and stared at the challenge that lay in front of us, my mind seemed sharp and focused. The travels of the day and the exasperating humidity made the river look not so ominous but inviting. It was like the river was calling for us. Every white-capped ripple was giving us a friendly wave to come in, which to me was a simple but reassuring sign that no harm would come to us. At least that was what my eyes and my head were telling me. But the pit of my stomach was telling me something else.

"All right," Felicia said somberly. "Now comes the hard part."

Once again, it was Samuel who decided to go first. He slowly stuck his dirty foot into the flowing water and gingerly put his weight on it. When he was able to bring his other foot in and stand sturdily in the river, he grew more confident. He took slow, lumbering steps toward the middle of the water, wading in until it was waist-high before turning back to us.

"It ain't too deep," he called out. "We can make it."

"You crazy?" I shouted back to him. "You can't swim!"

Samuel shook his head. "Nope," he agreed. "You can't neither. 'Sides . . . we ain't gonna swim it. We can walk it."

I exhaled slowly, staring down at the suddenly menacing river in front of me. Samuel was right. I couldn't swim. Georgeo had tried to teach me at one point, but it hadn't turned out so well. At that moment, I could clearly remember that day . . .

Georgeo had told me everything I needed to know. He'd said to lie flat, stick my face under the surface, and start paddling my arms like there was no tomorrow. When I dropped down into the water, I had done just that. I remember thrashing around in that river like I was trying to pummel it into submission. While I was swinging away, I remember feeling my right hand swing over and crack Georgeo right in the jaw. I'd popped up out of the water with a huge smile on my face, only to have it vanish as soon as I saw Georgeo on his back, slowly floating away from me with a dazed look on his face. Somehow, I had managed to pull him to the dry riverbank, but that had been my first—and last—swimming lesson. The only thing I had learned was that I had a heck of a knockout punch . . . as long as I wasn't looking.

Now, as I stood beside this powerful river with Felicia, I wished I had continued my lessons. They would have been excellent to fall back on.

"Come on!" Samuel shouted. "Before it gets too dark!"

I wrung my hands nervously. "I don't know."

"You want to get to that train, don't you?" he asked, staring intently at me.

Knowing he was right, I simply nodded.

"Good," he said. "I'll come back and you just take my hand. We'll all cross together, okay?"

I nodded once more, worried that my voice would crack if I tried to speak.

As promised, Samuel made his way back to Felicia and me, grabbing our hands before turning and practically dragging us into the river.

The water was shockingly cold. It felt like some kind of icy, electric chill that arced through my entire body, making me shiver as I continued into the deeper part.

"Be careful," Samuel said. "The rocks are pretty slippery."

He wasn't wrong. Already, with the current pushing against my legs and hips, my toes couldn't keep a steady grip on the bottom. The rocks were covered in a thin layer of algae that made the trek feel a bit like walking on ice. More than once, I would flail my arms as I was thrown off balance, a move that would threaten to drag Samuel and Felicia off their feet as well.

As we began to wade further into the depths of the river, the current was becoming more powerful by the second. I wasn't sure if any of us had the height or the body weight to make it completely across. As soon as the thought entered my mind, my right foot slipped fast off the surface of a rock, and I felt my body go horizontal on the surface of the water. I would have been dragged downstream if Samuel hadn't clamped his hand down hard on mine.

"It's too fast!" I screamed.

"Hold on!" he shouted back. On the other side of him, Felicia was beginning to wobble, as well. Samuel kept going, literally dragging both Felicia and me behind him. "Just don't let go of me!"

Felicia let out a panicked cry. "I'm slipping!"

Samuel only gritted his teeth. "Hold on!"

I was amazed at the strength of the river, the way it flowed around me, trying hard to pull me along with it. I tried to bring my legs back underneath me to stand again, but the water was just too overwhelming. All I could do was grab onto Samuel's hand with both of mine, feeling the cold white froth breaking against my head as I struggled to keep my mouth above the surface.

In front of me, Samuel reminded me much of my father, so determined and unrelenting. He kept his back to the current, letting the foaming rapids crash against him, flowing around his neck and over his shoulders. It looked almost like he was wearing the river itself, standing strong against its might with all of his. As Felicia finally lost her step, she could only mimic me, hanging onto Samuel as he alone continued across the river.

"I can't hold on!" Felicia cried.

"We're almost there!" Samuel replied.

Felicia's legs began to kick wildly next to me, threatening to knock me into the river's icy grasp. "I'm slipping!" she squealed.

Before Samuel or I could do anything, she was gone. The water took her so fast that I didn't even have time to offer her one of my hands. I tried to look behind me to see where she was headed, but all I could see was bubbling water. The rippling surface forced its way into my nostrils and ears.

"Felicia!" I shouted. "Felicia, no!"

With just me to hang on to, Samuel made faster progress across the middle of the river. When the water became shallower, I was able to take to my own feet once more and we both stumbled and hobbled out onto dry land. Immediately, the two of us broke into a dead run, heading in the same direction that Felicia had been swept by the current.

The river was littered with random logs and pieces of trees that it had dragged off the mountain as they came down. If she had hit any of these logs, if she'd knocked her head on one or become trapped beneath it . . . that would be the end. There would be nothing Samuel or I could do for her. We must have run over a hundred yards before we stopped suddenly at the sight of her.

Her body, soaking wet and unconscious, was nestled perfectly in the bare branches of a treetop that had become lodged between two large rocks. The branches hanging into the water acted as a net, and the current had simply pushed her up into them, keeping her safely out of the river's deadly reach. To our relief, the log wasn't far off the bank we were currently on. It took a fair bit of clever footwork to make it out to her, but Samuel was able to scoop her up beneath the arms and drag her back to the shallow water where I helped him haul her up onto the grass.

As soon as we tilted her onto her side, water spewed from her mouth and she gave a violent cough, spraying the grass with moisture as it exploded from her lungs. For a moment, she could only lie there, coughing and convulsing, sucking in shallow breaths as I clutched her hand tightly and Samuel thumped his hand on her back the way Ma used to do when we drank water too fast in the field.

"You're okay," Samuel said to her, his voice calm and soothing. "Just breathe. You're okay."

As I ran a hand through my bushy hair to shake the water droplets from it, I turned to look at the log that had saved my sister's life. The naked, jagged branches still dipped into water, pointing downward at a diagonal angle. If Felicia had been even a little bit under the surface, those tree limbs would have skewered her like a spear tip. If she had been a little bit to the right or the left, those big rocks would have knocked her out for good. She had come to the tree at the perfect angle . . . at the perfect speed.

To me, it was a miracle. Never will I ever be convinced otherwise. That tree seemed like it had been placed there for the sole purpose of saving a young girl lost in the current. Like a giant hand from the heavens had known in advance what was going to happen and the branches were its fingers, plucking her out of the water, where Samuel and I could reach her. It was meant to be. No doubt in my mind. I began to believe, then . . . that we were meant to go on. There was something more important in store for us. I knew that fate, God, whatever you'd like to call it, needed us, needed Felicia for something else. She had another purpose, I was sure of it. At the time, I couldn't guess as to what, but I couldn't shake the feeling that we'd just had a brush with the fine threads of destiny . . . and now we were all firmly tangled within it.

With Felicia finally opening her eyes, I crouched down beside her and Samuel. "Maybe we should stay here for the night," I suggested.

Felicia let out a gurgling laugh. "Good plan."

Chapter 6

As he walked, Sheriff Dobson dabbed at the back of his neck with a yellow-stained rag, wiping the dirt and sweat that had accumulated there from the heat. Through his thinning white hair, Slate could also see his scalp glistening with perspiration. The Sheriff was a very rotund man. Rather than walking, he waddled into the doors of the Alexandria city jail, his shoulders thrown back in an attempt to puff out his chest. All it did was allow his ample belly to stick out even further. Slate immediately disliked the man. He breathed too hard. He smelled worse than the slaves in the field, and he seemed of frustratingly dull intelligence. Fortunately, Slate's dealings with the small-town "lawman" would be short-lived.

It hadn't taken long for Slate and his men to end up here. They hadn't even needed to visit a rail yard. The scent dogs had sniffed their way through the thick forest outside the plantation and ended up at some railroad tracks for a Southbound train. Slate wasn't sure if the kids had knowingly tried to run further South or if it was just an accident, but the footprints in the gravel were undeniable. The train had definitely come this way. The first stop after they'd boarded was Alexandria, and Slate's hunch about checking the train depot had led him here . . . and was hopefully about to provide the information he needed.

He followed Dobson into the white-painted city jail and lifted the tinted lenses from his eyes. The first thing that hit him was the smell. It was dank mildew and raw sewage, combined in an odor that was strong enough to make his eyes begin watering. The reception area was dark and had a general griminess to it, but it wouldn't account for such a stench. Slate wondered how many men were locked in the holding cells. The few desks and tables in the room were mostly empty, giving Slate the impression that a lot of the things that happened here weren't documented. Across the small room, another grey-haired man, a Deputy—this one tall and gangly—sat at a plain wooden desk, fanning himself with his brimmed hat. Peering over the top of his newspaper, his jaw absent-mindedly worked back and forth as he eyed Slate with curiosity. The Sheriff must have seen it, too. He raised his plump fist to his lips and cleared his throat.

"Uh . . . County Inspector," Dobson huffed. "Come to make sure the cells are secure." It was brief and vague, but it was enough of a lie to get the Deputy to nod his head, showing he understood.

It had been surprisingly easy to bribe information out of Sheriff Dobson. A few dollars in his palm and he was giving up everything he knew about the arrest at the train yard. He even volunteered to show Slate to the prisoner whom he had locked up the previous night. Every man had his price, it was true, but the fact that Dobson's was so low practically forbade Slate from giving him any respect at all.

As the two men made their way through reception and into the holding cells, Slate was sorely tempted to raise his handkerchief to his nose. The smell was unholy. As he passed cell after cell, he could see why. These conditions were horrible. Every man in a cell looked as though he had been there for quite some time. Vagrants, Union sympathizers, escaped slaves waiting to be picked up by their masters or sold to the highest bidder, all of them were left filthy and unshaven with nothing but a bucket in the corner to use as a toilet. Several of them sported bloody gashes on their bodies or swollen lumps on their heads. Upon seeing the Sheriff coming, the inmates' faces begin to contort in sudden fear. This led Slate to conclude that Dobson and his deputies must make a habit of beating their prisoners. Finally, at the end of the long hallway, the Sheriff stopped outside the final cell, using his rag to wipe off his heavy brow.

"Right there's the one we brought in last night," Dobson said, pointing through the bars. "He was on the train that came through. One o' my boys, Lloyd, saw him hoppin' out of an empty car and brought him in. Name's Seth, or so he says."

Slate drew a deep breath, trying his best to ignore the ubiquitous odor, and narrowed his eyes at the man in the cell. He was as dirty and haggard as any man Slate had ever seen. His stringy hair was long and unkempt, his ashen skin covered in dirt and mud, among other things, and his tattered clothes hung loosely off his frail body. This man had been wandering for quite some time.

"Can he talk?" Slate asked. If any of the other prisoners were any indication, this man could very well have suffered a concussion by now.

Dobson nodded. "Yep. Been asking for a drink all morning. Only shut up a few hours ago."

Slate raised his eyebrow. "Is that so?"

Dobson nodded, wiping himself down again. "Yessir. Too much shine. He's dryin' out cold turkey . . . and it ain't pretty."

As Slate looked closer, he could see that the man was shivering, despite the heat of the day. His hands were clenched into fists and his blackened toes were curled as far as they could go. Dobson was right.

"Thank you, Sheriff," Slate said, giving Dobson a clear dismissal.

"I'll, uh . . . leave you to it," Dobson said, nodding. With a sigh, he turned and began waddling back the way they had come, whistling loudly as if he hadn't a care in the world. When he had rounded the corner and gone, Slate turned his attention back to the man in the cell.

"Seth," he said firmly. "I got questions that need answering."

The ragged man named Seth gave no response. If he was conscious, he gave no such indication.

"The Sheriff tells me you were on that train last night," Slate continued, feeling his patience quickly leaching out of him. "Were you alone?"

Seth said nothing.

Clenching his teeth, Slate hammered his palm into the steel bars, making them clang loudly against their wooden bracings. "Who else was on that train?" he bellowed loudly. "Tell me!"

Despite the noise, Seth gave no reaction whatsoever. He didn't even register that anyone was speaking to him. Slate was suddenly very tempted to stomp his way back to the Sheriff and get the keys to the cell. Maybe a few kicks to the ribs would loosen the vagabond's tongue. Before he stepped away, however, he had a different thought, one that would require much less time and effort.

"You know," he said, reaching into his vest pocket, "You look like a man who appreciates a good whiskey. Am I right, Seth?" From his vest, he pulled a tall metal flask, filled to the brim with spirits from his own personal stores.

As he had predicted, Seth slowly rolled forward and put his thin arms underneath him, turning his head to look over at Slate. His eyes immediately locked onto the flask and Slate could see the mad desperation suddenly wash over him. Like a man possessed, he scrambled forward on his hands and knees, stretching his fingers out for the flask just as Slate pulled it out of his reach.

"Whoa, easy there!" Slate said, his voice high and condescending. "Let's not be hasty, now. I still have some questions for you."

Seth's sweat-covered face contorted into one that looked almost like grief. His eyes never left the metal flask.

Just to make his work easier, Slate unscrewed the cap and held the opening up to his nose, drawing in a deep breath with overstated relish. "Smells good. Aged 12 years in an oak barrel.

Smooth and warm . . . like a good whiskey should be."

Seth was practically licking his lips. He looked alarmingly like a dog as he sat back on his heels, as if waiting for a treat from his master.

"You want a taste pretty bad, don't ya?" Slate said, giving the flask a small shake, sloshing the liquid inside.

Seth nodded enthusiastically.

"Then you tell me," Slate said darkly, leaning toward the steel bars. "Where did they go?"

For the first time, Seth's gaze traveled up to meet Slate's and his grey eyes were already full of remorse. Slate knew his plan had worked.

"You know who I'm talking about," he said. "Those runaways! Where are they? Where did they get off?"

Seth swallowed hard, bringing his filthy hands up to cover his face in shame as he sat in front of the cell bars.

Slate gave him a few seconds to respond, but all he could seem to do was sob into his dirty fingers. "The longer you wait, Seth . . . well . . ." He slowly tilted the flask sideways, allowing a tiny bit of the whiskey to trickle out onto the disgusting stone floor.

"Wait!" Seth screamed. "Wait! Don't do that! Please!"

Slate hunkered down outside the bars, rattling the flask gingerly in his hands. "You can have it all," he said softly. "*If* you have something to tell me."

Seth wiped his nose on the back if his hand, but didn't respond.

"You do have something to tell me," Slate prodded. "Don't you?"

Drawing in a shaky breath, Seth closed his eyes, letting new tears roll down his cheeks as he slowly nodded his head.

***   ***   ***

"We really should find something to eat," Samuel said as we trudged through the rocky foothills of the mountain. The green and gold fields were behind us now, and we were beginning to make our climb up the increasingly steep slopes. Unfortunately, we hadn't had anything to eat since we left the plantation, and all of our stomachs were aching badly with hunger.

"Just try not to think about it," Felicia said. I knew she was trying not to complain, but the look on her face told me that she was fretting just as much as Samuel. For her, I was also doing my best not to whine about my empty belly. It didn't do anyone any good. If anything, it just made us all feel even more miserable. Samuel, on the other hand, couldn't seem to let it go.

"We shoulda tried to catch some fish at the river back there," he said, panting for breath.

I shook my head, wiping sweat from my face with the back of my hand. "Nothing to catch 'em with."

"We got our hands, ain't we?" he protested.

"We'll find something," Felicia chimed in, sounding as cheerful as possible despite the weary look about her. "Don't you worry."

Pausing to take a few deep breaths, I looked over at my sister, suddenly very glad that she was still here. Maybe it hadn't totally sunk in yet, but I reminded myself that she very nearly died the day before. We almost lost her. By the good Lord's grace, we didn't, and I was very grateful for that.

"Ya know," I started simply to her, "I'm glad you're still with us."

She gave me a genuine smile and nodded her head before hopping over a rock. "Yeah, me too."

"You feeling okay?" I asked. I'm not sure if I was asking for her sake or for my own peace of mind. Probably a little of both.

Felicia let out a weary chuckle. "Don't you worry, Isaac. I'm fine."

I nodded. "So . . . you're feeling fast, then?"

With a mischievous grin, she stopped and turned to me. "Yeah, I think I'm feeling pretty fast."

"How fast?"

"Fast enough to catch your lazy butt!" she shouted merrily, jogging toward me.

I turned and began to run from her, doing my best to follow the contours of the hills without tripping on rocks or bushes. "Prove it!" I hollered back to her. "Catch me if you can!"

I led her on a winding path up the hill slope in a familiar game of freeze tag, both of us ignoring the hunger in our bellies and the pain in our feet. She laughed loudly as I stumbled and couldn't get up. For once, it was I—not she—who displayed a moment of clumsiness.

My misstep had allowed her to be within striking distance as her hand quickly reached towards me. "Gotcha!" she exclaimed, tagging me on the back. I stiffened straight, acting like I had been suddenly frozen solid. "No! Samuel! Samuel, unfreeze me! Quick!"

A few yards away, a visibly exhausted Samuel glared at us. "I don't think this is the time to be playin'." he said sternly.

"Unfreeze me!" I said, feigning urgency.

"Both of you come back here!" he yelled. "Lord knows what's around these parts! Best stick together!"

Rolling my eyes at him, I unfroze myself and took off after Felicia. "Samuel's being a baby! I'm coming after you!"

Felicia giggled wildly as I took off after her. As I ran, my lungs couldn't seem to get enough air into them. It seemed our lack of food had sapped more of my energy than I'd thought it would. Even so, I had to disagree with Samuel. I thought it was as good a time as any to be playing. I knew it would be the last chance for quite a while to have some actual fun, so I wasn't keen on letting the opportunity pass me by. So, with my lungs and ribs aching with every breath, I kept on going, smiling and laughing as I felt the warm air rushing across my sweat-covered skin and through my wild hair. Within a few seconds, I had caught up to Felicia and tagged her back. Drained as I was, my speed was still something to be reckoned with.

She took a moment to catch a few breaths and allowed me to bolt away from her. Seizing the opportunity for a victory, I tried to put as much distance between us as I could. I summoned as much willpower as possible and charged straight up the ridge we were climbing, laughing gleefully as I crested the hill and stepped onto a plateau.

That first step was my only one, though.

I stopped immediately, my labored breath catching somewhere deep in my throat. When it finally returned to me, it brought with it the faint, lingering odors of blood and gunpowder. The smells weren't that strong, but the sight that accompanied them was what stopped me in my tracks. My eyes were wide with shock and horror, and I could only stare out across the wide plateau, wondering just what had happened.

"You ain't supposed to freeze till I tag you, dummy!" Felicia trilled as she dashed up behind me. "Gotcha!"

Even her hard slap on the shoulder wasn't enough to divert my attention. Beside me, however, I did notice that Felicia had also stopped to look upon the ghastly sight.

"Oh . . ." she muttered. It sounded like an involuntary noise.

Behind us, Samuel finally came huffing and puffing up to the hillcrest. "Whatcha looking at?" He asked, stumbling up next to me. Just like Felicia and me, he stopped short when his eyes fell upon the hundreds of dead men who lay in the short grass before us.

I don't know when exactly the battle had taken place, but it couldn't have been more than a day or two. I had seen dead bodies before, but they were usually old horses that had to be put down, even the occasional field worker who dropped dead from heat exhaustion or an infected lash wound. In a few days' time, the bodies would get so swelled up that they looked like balloons. After that, the stink would get really bad. None of the bodies before me now had reached that level of decay. They still seemed relatively fresh, like the battle had just ended. A part of me was wondering when exactly it *had* come to an end, but I realized that it didn't make much of a difference.

There were men from both sides of the war lying at my feet. Navy blue Union uniforms, grey jackets and tattered outfits, they all blended together in a breathtaking patchwork of death that spread out for a hundred yards in every direction. Aside from the blue and grey, the color that caught my attention most was the red, the blood that covered many of their faces and hands, stained their coats and guns. It wasn't just men that lay broken and wrecked on the plateau. There were several dogs and horses that had also paid the ultimate price. I don't know why exactly, but the only thing I could feel at that moment was disappointment.

To my right, Felicia cleared her throat, pulling her eyes away from the scene. "Come on," she said somberly. "We need to keep going."

Neither Samuel nor I moved an inch from where we stood. It was like we were hypnotized by the atrocities before us. We couldn't tear our eyes away from it, like the spell of death had washed over us, keeping our weary feet rooted to the ground.

"Come *on,*" Felicia urged. "In a few hours, it'll be gettin' dark. We gotta cover more ground if we're gonna make it to Chesterfield in time. Come on, now."

"We could use a gun," Samuel said, his voice flat and emotionless. His eyes were fixed on the man nearest to us, a young Confederate soldier who still clutched his musket in his cold hands.

"No!" Felicia snapped. "We ain't taking nothing from any of these men."

"Why not?" Samuel asked, finally turning his head to look at her. "We could use it to get some food! Or fight off anyone that tries to hurt us!"

"No, Samuel!" Felicia shouted adamantly. "These men died fighting for their honor. We ain't gonna disrespect that by robbing 'em of their belongings! Now, come on! Both of you! We gotta go!"

Muttering angrily under his breath, Samuel trudged after her as she made to take the long way around the battlefield. As he went, Samuel stopped at the nearest dead horse and pulled a large canvas bag from off its back.

"Horses don't have no belongings," he grumbled, slinging the bag over his shoulder. "Maybe it has some food in here."

Finally, I was able to move my feet. The spell had worn off and I lowered my eyes to the bloodstained grass, trotting after Samuel and Felicia. As we went, though, I couldn't help but look out over the expanse of corpses. The ground was literally covered in them. It was so much death, the likes of which I had never seen before. My young mind couldn't really make sense of it. Lying in the grass, there weren't any Confederate soldiers or Union soldiers, there were only men. Some were young, some were old, but all of them had given their lives and it had done nothing. Nothing had come of it. Nothing had been solved.

I couldn't understand it.

The rest of the day passed in relative silence. All of our minds were still on the gruesome discovery we had made on that plateau. We journeyed on for several long miles, up the rolling foothills and into the forested region of the mountain itself. We discovered that we didn't need to go completely over it, which was a relief, but only across the lower slope. With any luck, we would be on the other side my nightfall tomorrow.

It turned out that Samuel had made the right decision in taking that pack from the dead horse. It contained five water canteens, some cooking pans, a few tins of hardtack, sugar, and coffee, and a large wool blanket that we were all currently huddled under. The forest floor was damp on our backs and the higher elevation made the air surprisingly cool for summertime. With the blanket, though, we were able to smash together and keep warm. The hardtack was a welcome sight. We ate plenty of it back on the plantation, and this stuff was just the same. It looked like bread, but it felt and tasted like you were eating a brick. When we stopped for the evening, we ate every bit of it, using generous amounts of the sugar to improve the flavor of it. Now, with our bellies full and satisfied, we had come to rest under the thick branches of an old oak tree.

On either side of me, Felicia and Samuel were fast sleep, their breathing slow and heavy as they dreamed on. Unfortunately, the night was not so kind to me. With my fingers laced behind my head, I lay there on the forest floor, staring up into the heavens. I couldn't seem to get the sight of those dead soldiers out of my mind. Even the stars reminded me of them, all strewn about on and on without any rhyme or reason. Just like those bodies had been. I thought of the young man that Samuel had wanted to steal from. I could see his face so clearly in my head. The closed eyes, the open mouth, and the dried blood that had pooled from the hole in his neck . . . I couldn't seem to block it out. I found myself wondering who that young man had been. What was his name? What made him join up to fight in the war? Where was his family? Did they know he had died? Or would they be fretting in front of a hearth somewhere, waiting for a letter or a visit that would never come?

It was a strange feeling, grieving for a man I didn't know, for a whole field of men I didn't know. How sad and heartbroken all of their families must be, to be wishing for the best, hoping that their loved one will be all right and come home. It wasn't long before my thoughts drifted to my own family that I had left behind: my mother and father. Where were they right now? Still at the plantation? Were they all right? I tried to send my thoughts out to them, hoping they wouldn't be as sad as the families of those soldiers. I hoped they wouldn't worry too much about us.

With a sigh, I silently bid them goodnight and rolled onto my side, trying my best to think of something else besides dead soldiers.

*** *** ***

Outside of her cabin, Elizabeth's weary shoulders gave a shudder as the cool night air brushed along the back of her neck. As she slowly tipped back and forth in her old rocking chair, she ran her dry hands over the skin of her arms, trying to soothe away the goose flesh that had sprouted there. In front of her, a single firefly shined brightly as it buzzed upward in an erratic pattern. Elizabeth's eyes followed it up and up, over the cotton shrubs, over the distant trees, until she lost it amidst the radiant twinkling of the stars. As she stared up at them longingly, she got the sensation that somewhere—maybe near, maybe far—her children were looking at the same stars. She felt the urge to call out to them, to sing to those bright, glimmering pearls in the sky. They felt closer tonight, as if she could reach out her arm and grab a handful of them to keep and admire. With a sigh, she simply resigned herself to continue rocking, hoping that they knew how much she loved them.

Duke's slow, heavy footsteps sounded on the old floorboards of the cabin as he strolled out to the porch to stand beside her. With his hands stuffed in the pockets of his trousers, he followed Elizabeth's gaze up into the heavens, trying his best to find what she was seeing. A few long minutes passed as they stared skyward. The crickets in the fields chirped loudly to fill the silence.

Finally, Duke lowered his head and scratched his thick beard, glancing over at Elizabeth.

"Whatcha thinkin' about, Mama?" he asked softly, his words heavy with concern.

Elizabeth gave a tiny smile. "Same thing you are." She replied.

Duke nodded, exhaling loudly. "Yeah. They's good kids, though. They're gonna do all right." He looked over his shoulder and into the door of the cabin. "Place sure is quiet now. Lotta empty beds in there."

From the corner of her eye, Elizabeth could see the deep lines of worry that had formed on Duke's brow as he stared out over the field. "Don't fret," she said soothingly. "We raised 'em up good. They will be fine, Duke."

He nodded, working his jaw back and forth. "Yeah," he said quietly. "Just fine."

From the dirt path that led to the plantation house, loud footfalls could be heard sprinting up toward the cabins. Someone was running down as fast as they could from the house. This would have been odd in the daytime, but at this time of night, it was very disconcerting. Elizabeth stood from her chair, stepping up beside Duke as a dark figure dashed around the front of their cabin and stopped at the porch steps.

"Blue!" Duke exclaimed, keeping his voice hushed. "What on earth you doin'?"

Blue was doubled over in front of the porch, his shoulders heaving with every labored breath.

He had been running for all he was worth. Elizabeth wondered what would have got him in such a state.

"Duke," Blue wheezed. "I come as quick as I could!"

"Catch your breath, my friend," Duke said, cracking a bit of a smile. "You're getting out of shape in your old age."

Standing straight, Blue shook his head. "The train. The train don't go North anymore. It don't go North."

The playful smile on Duke's face evaporated instantly. "What you talkin' about, Blue? You be straight with me, now." His tone was almost threatening, something that Elizabeth wasn't fond of hearing.

Blue held up his hands. "No disrespect, Duke. I'm just tellin' you what I know. My uncle used to work repairing the railroad. I told him about the track you were at and he says it don't go North, anymore. Not since the war."

Duke took a heavy step forward, closing the distance between him and his friend. "Where . . . does it go?" he asked. His words were slow and measured as he tried to control the sudden well of emotions that were burning in his dark eyes.

Blue just shook his head, his face showing a mix of pain and remorse.

"Where does it go?!" Duke shouted, his hands balling into fists.

"It goes South, Duke," Blue said morosely. "It goes further South. The train that your kids stole a ride from was going further South."

"South?" Elizabeth asked, her voice high with sudden panic. "Where South?"

"Way down," Blue said sadly. "Where the war is the worst."

For several seconds, Duke said nothing. He didn't react at all. He simply stood in place, his wide eyes boring into Blue, searching for any hint of deception. When he found none, he suddenly sprinted into the cabin, leaving Elizabeth staring after him.

"What are you doing?" she asked, heading toward the door. Before she could reach it, Duke was already bolting out of it, trying to walk and pull his shoes on at the same time.

"Duke!" she called, suddenly on the verge of tears.

"I have to go find them!" he said, bending down to tie his laces.

Elizabeth stepped off the porch, feeling the dry dirt sifting between her toes. "Duke, you can't leave!"

"Food," he said, turning and dashing back into the cabin.

"Listen to me!" Elizabeth shrieked at him, trying desperately to get him to hear her out. She stepped in front of the cabin door as he was trying to make his way out.

"I ain't got time to listen!" Duke shouted as he muscled past her. "I gotta go find our kids! I gotta make sure they're safe!"

Elizabeth looked up into his eyes, her lips trembling. "If you go, Duke, Master Tomstin will put your punishment on every child in these fields! Every one of them!"

With a loud groan, Duke threw his hands up in the air, stepping off the porch once more. "I don't have time for this! Our children need saving!"

With all her might, Elizabeth caught his arm and spun him around to face her. "Stop! Tomstin will *kill* for what you're about to do! You hear me? He'll kill one of these kids in these other cabins! Maybe more and you know it! Those are other people's babies that you're putting in danger! Are you prepared to live with that? Because I'm not!"

"She's right, Duke," Blue said timidly. "Tomstin ain't gonna let this one go."

Elizabeth turned to him. In the heat of the moment, she had forgotten he was there. Now, she gave him a nod of thanks for taking her side. Duke needed as many voices of reason as he could get.

"You know I'm right," Elizabeth said, turning back to look up at Duke. "If you go, everyone will feel the pain of it."

As she spoke, she couldn't fight the tears from rolling down her cheeks. The moistness of Duke's eyes mirrored her own, and she knew she had gotten through to him. He looked down at her, his eyebrows pulled so far together that they looked almost like one.

"What would you have me do, Mama?" he asked softly.

Elizabeth sniffled and placed her hand on Duke's broad shoulder. "We put them into the hands of the Lord," she whispered to him. "We need to trust Him now."

Duke reached up and grasped her small hand in his, holding it to his lips as he fought the tears of frustration. "But, they're my babies."

Elizabeth moved into him, wrapping her free arm around his waist. "They're mine, too," she said, giving him a squeeze. "Like I said . . . we raised 'em right. They're good kids. They can take care of themselves, darling. They are still alive and well, I know it."

Duke closed his eyes, letting out a slow breath through his nose. His face had lost all of the fire that had just been burning in it. It had been replaced by a sluggish exhaustion. "How do you know?" he asked mournfully, looking down at her for reassurance.

Placing her hand over her heart, Elizabeth gave him the most genuine smile that she could muster. "Because I just know. I feel them."

Duke nodded, his head and shoulders hanging low in defeat. "Okay," he murmured. "I'll stay."

Chapter 7

None of us had slept much. With the soggy ground and cool night air, there wasn't much comfort to be had. The blanket that Samuel had got from the dead horse had probably saved our lives, but it didn't do much more than that. The sun was rising higher, making the air a little bit warmer as it went. Hopefully, it would dry out our clothes and help us walk without our arms wrapped around ourselves. I wasn't in the greatest of moods, unfortunately. Neither were Felicia and Samuel. Our father had planned far enough ahead to know where and when to take us to the tracks, but he hadn't thought to make sure we had food or water? Even a jacket of some kind? He had basically dragged us out of bed in the middle of the night and thrown us into the wild with just the clothes on our backs. What kind of a plan was that? He had wanted us to succeed, but he had stacked the odds completely against us. Thinking about it upset me at first but then I realized that my father's faith might have played a part in his lack of preparation. You see, he believed and always taught us that God will provide. And in some odd way, He had—at least up until now.

As my mind was pondering upon these thoughts, my ears began to tingle as they were suddenly filled with the sounds of nature around us. There were so many things in this forest that I had never experienced before. There were bird songs that I had never heard. There were tiny animals scurrying through the undergrowth that I had never laid eyes on, even the sight of a pine tree growing in a natural setting. I'd seen a few every year around Christmastime when Master Tomstin would have them hauled to his house. They always smelled fine from a distance, but up close, they smelled wonderful. Everything in the forest did. The pine needles, the cedar, the wet dirt itself, they were all part of a heavenly potpourri that I was very much in love with. As my siblings and I continued slowly hiking up the steep slope of the mountain, I began to hear another noise I wasn't familiar with. It was some kind of grunting, low and guttural, like a field worker trying to pull a stuck plow out of the dirt.

I chanced a glance at my brother and sister, noticing that they had the same confused look that I felt manifesting on my own face. "What's that sound?" I asked.

Felicia stood on her toes, trying her best to see above the foliage around us. "I don't know," she said. "I can't tell."

As we continued walking, the ground surface began to level out, which meant that we had finally reached the ridge of the mountain and would soon be going down the other side. The further we went, the closer we got to the odd grunting noise. As the terrain became smoother and less perilous, we suddenly began to feel nervous about approaching whatever it was that was making the sound. The grunting was louder and angrier now, and there was only a small row of bushes that obscured our view of the culprit. Hesitating, we stopped behind it for a few seconds before Felicia reach forward and slowly parted the leaves in front of us. As we all crowded our heads together, we looked past the thick leaves and into the small clearing beyond.

There, just in front of us, a thick, crooked tree stood alone. In a hollow in the center of the trunk, an enormous beehive was buzzing with activity. Also hanging onto the trunk, a black bear was hungrily stuffing his face with honey, reaching his thick paw into the hive again and again to get more. It seemed we had discovered the source of the grunting and growling. I had never seen a bear before. I can't even remember where I had learned of them, but as soon as I set my eyes on it, I knew what it was. I also knew how very deadly they could be. I would have likely been scared stiff if it wasn't for the honey.

"That looks real good," Samuel said in a hushed voice, his eyes locked on the tree's hollow.

"Don't it, though?" Felicia agreed.

I couldn't deny that they were right. All that fresh, sticky-sweet honey did sound very delicious, especially considering we had eaten the last of the meager hardtack about eighteen hours previous. It was funny how we all suddenly found the ability to ignore the obvious threat of the bear just because there was something edible within reach. We didn't even see the bear, really . . . all we could see was that sweet honey. I knew hunger was a powerful force, but I had never known the full extent of it until that day. I'd be lying if I said my mouth wasn't watering just at the thought of it. I cast another glance at Felicia and Samuel. From the ravenous looks on their faces, they were thinking the same thing I was. We needed that honey.

"We gotta get us some of that," Samuel said, his voice still subdued.

"Yeah," Felicia said with a nod. "But, that bear's gotta go. Soon. Or there won't be anything left for us."

Cracking a wide grin, I looked over at her. "What are you plannin' on doing? Ask him to leave?"

Felicia frowned. "I don't think asking him's gonna do it."

For a few seconds, the three of us simply stood there, watching the bear continue to try and dig out as much of the bees' honey as he could. Finally, Felicia couldn't take anymore. Slapping her thighs in frustration, she turned to Samuel and seized him by the shoulder, pulling him toward her.

"Okay, Samuel," she said in a whisper. "Either you or me has gotta go pick a fight with that bear. We gotta get him so mad that he decides to chase us instead. That way, the other two can gather up some honey while the bear is gone."

Samuel turned his head back to the bear and pursed his lips to the side, thinking hard. "Pick a fight, huh?"

"Are you two plumb crazy?" I hissed, doing my best to keep from shouting. "It's a bear! It could kill all three of us in ten seconds, probably!"

Felicia shook her head, looking out at the animal. "Nah, come on. He ain't even that big. Look at him."

Reflexively, I darted my eyes over to the bear. She was right. He wasn't very big. He looked only a couple of inches bigger than I was, which would put him at about five feet tall, or so. He must have been pretty young, not yet fully grown. Even so, I didn't want Felicia or Samuel to go messing around with that beast. If they could get it to chase them, what then? Samuel wasn't fast enough and Felicia would surely trip over something and fall down. I didn't help pull her from a river just so she could get devoured by a hungry animal.

"See?" Felicia went on. "He's not big at all. I've seen dogs bigger than him."

"He still has claws and teeth," I countered.

Felicia smiled. "He's also got a belly full of honey. He'll only chase me for a minute before he gets tired and quits, I'll betcha anything. I always get winded easy after I eat. Don't you?"

I chewed my tongue as I stared at the bear. She had a point. All that was needed was a couple of minutes to distract it while the other two dug some honey out of the beehive. The thought suddenly brought up another concern.

"What about the bees?" I asked, noticing several of them feebly trying to annoy the bear away. My eyesight being a bit fuzzy and all, there may very well have been a hundred more around that tree.

Samuel shook his head at my question. "There's only a few," he said.

"The others are probably out getting more honey," Felicia suggested. "Or they just gave up and left. Besides, I'll gladly put up with a few bee stings if I can get me some honey out of the deal."

I had to admit . . . she had a point. As I stared at the sweet, golden honey slowly dripping down the tree trunk, I suddenly believed wholeheartedly that her plan would work. We just had to distract that bear. But, I still couldn't forget the fact that Samuel was too slow and Felicia was too clumsy. Neither of them would be able to pull it off.

With a determined look on her face, Felicia bent down and scooped up a thin twig from the forest floor and snapped it in half, stuffing both ends into her closed fist. "Okay," she said, turning to Samuel. "Draw one. Whoever has the shorter one gets to go."

I didn't get to see who drew the short stick, though. I was already moving. Without a word, I slipped through the bushes and was tiptoeing my way toward the growling bear, doing my very best to stay light on my feet. Already, the adrenaline was tingling through me, making every breath shorter and more ragged. I don't know what I was thinking, other than I knew I wanted some sugary sweetness to eat.

I guess every boy has to prove his manhood at some point in his life. Some do it by showing off strength, some do it by kissing the prettiest girl around, like Samuel. But me, I had to go and pick a fight with a bear. Though, now that I was exposed and vulnerable against a deadly animal, I couldn't help but wish there were a pretty girl to kiss instead.

From behind the bushes, Samuel crept toward me. "Isaac! Get back here!"

Without looking back at him, I shook my head. He must have taken the hint, because that was the last protest I heard from him. I was on my own for now. It was up to me to get that bear down from the tree. I was the only one fast enough to keep it distracted while Felicia and Samuel got the honey.

"Okay, woolly bear," I said stepping up to the tree. "It's just you and me. Come on and get me!"

For a short second, the bear completely stopped what it was doing and turned its honey-coated face toward me, taking a few moments to appraise me before sticking its paw back into the beehive.

"Hey!" I shouted. "I'm talkin' to you! Come and get me, dummy!"

This time, the bear seemed to care even less about me. He didn't even slow down licking his paw. I may as well have been one of the insignificant bees buzzing around him. I realized

I was going to have to up my game if I was going to get that stubborn bear off that honey.

I lowered my gaze and scanned the ground around me. Pinecones would do no good. I could poke it with a stick, but that sort of seemed like suicide. Finally, my eyes fell upon a cluster of rocks. In truth, it looked like just one bigger rock that had been broken into pieces, but either way, it would do nicely. Without wasting any time, I bent down and grasped a decent-sized chunk and hurled it right at the bear, watching with satisfaction as it glanced off its meaty shoulder. Once again, the animal looked down at me for a few seconds before returning to its task.

"Unbelievable!" I shouted, grabbing a second rock. I put more muscle into the throw than last time, smiling as it thumped hard into a hind leg.

To my surprise, the bear stopped what it was doing, turned its head, and hissed at me, sounding like an enormous, angry cat. I blinked up at the beast, surprised by its strange behavior. To my dismay, though, he continued to look at me for a moment and then just went right on grabbing for the honey.

"All right, that's it!" I said in frustration. With a sudden boldness burning through me, I grasped the largest rock of the bunch and clutched it in my fist. The thing had to weigh at least five pounds. With this boulder landing right in its honey-filled belly, I was sure I'd get its attention. So, with my newfound determination, I cranked back my arm and put everything I had into the throw, yelling loudly as I hurled it far and fast.

Unfortunately, it sailed too far and too fast. Instead of landing in his big belly, the rock went all the way up and cracked the bear directly in the side of his furry head, knocking the poor thing out instantaneously. I could only watch, eyes wide with shock, as the limp body of the bear toppled backward through the air and landed in a heap on the forest floor.

For a long minute, there was no sound. I wasn't even sure *I* was breathing. The bear hitting the ground was like a gunshot going off, silencing everything and everyone around it. I'm not positive how long we all stood in place, but eventually, Felicia and Samuel made their way over to me.

"Wow!" Samuel said, smiling wide. "Nice shot!"

I swallowed hard. "Oh, what have I done?" I said quietly, taking a step toward the bear, which still had not moved at all. "I think I killed it."

Samuel scoffed. "Nah, just knocked him out, is all. Give him a tap on the nose and wake him up. You'll see."

"Don't do that," Felicia said, a scolding tone in her voice. "Let him sleep, if that's what he's doing. We gotta get this honey before he wakes up."

I scurried over to the motionless bear as Samuel shrugged off his pack and held out his hands for Felicia to put her foot in. "Come on," he said to her. "I'll give you a boost."

As they busied themselves with the remains of the beehive, I knelt down beside my woolly victim, feeling all kinds of guilt pummeling at my insides. Despite all my common sense telling me that it was a terrible idea to wake an animal that could easily rip my face off, I gave the bear a shake. "Come on," I said. "Don't be dead. I just didn't want you eating all the honey!" It occurred to me that I was trying to apologize to a creature that wouldn't have been able to understand me even if it had been conscious, so I resorted to tapping its nose like Samuel had instructed. I still knew it would be a bad idea to wake the bear, but I mostly just wanted to make sure it was still alive. I knew I would feel awful if I had killed it by accident.

From behind me, Felicia shouted down from atop Samuel's shoulders. "Isaac, you keep your eyes on that thing! If it starts to wake up, you be sure and yell for us!"

"Okay," I answered monotonously. I gave the nose a few more taps, but there was no response.

I couldn't even see its chest rising and falling. It let out a small, cough-like sound, and I put my ear to its belly to see if I could hear a heartbeat. Before I could focus enough to hear anything, I felt a sudden hot blast of air on the back of my head. My eyeballs immediately went wide. Slowly, as to not make any sudden movements, I lifted my head off the bear's stomach and turned toward its face, only to see it staring back at me with a look in its eye that I could only describe as "confused anger."

The bear gave a loud huff, flexing its body so that it could roll upright. I took the opportunity to scramble backward and get to my own feet. They were trembling underneath me, like they were trying to run even before I had told them to.

"He's not dead!" I shouted, suddenly wondering if I could make it up one of the surrounding trees before I was mauled to death. In front of me, the bear gave an intimidating growl and hopped up on its hind legs, drawing to its full height before letting out a spine-chilling roar that set every hair on my body on end. I had been wrong when I estimated it to only stand a few inches higher than I did. As I looked up at it in bewilderment, that bear seemed like it was ten feet tall.

"Isaac, get your butt outta there!" Felicia screamed.

I didn't have to be told twice. I took several steps back, my face still frozen in disbelief. The bear gave a momentary glance to Samuel and Felicia, but it turned its attention right back to me. I think it knew I had whacked it with the rock . . . and it wanted revenge. With another terrifying growl, the bear set forward on all fours and charged right for me. I didn't even see it take its second step, though. I was already running.

"It was an accident!" I yelped as I tore through the shrubs and foliage. For some reason, trying to reason with a wild animal seemed like as good an idea as any at the time. Of course, it had no effect. I ran the equivalent of the cotton field itself, looking behind me every few steps to make sure the bear wasn't catching me. I knew I was fast, but I also didn't have four legs. With that hairy monster chasing after me, grunting and snarling and wanting me for lunch, I don't think I have ever been so petrified in my life!

I've heard plenty of people over the years talk about having superhuman experiences, like being able to cut off their own arm to survive being stuck in something, or running into a burning building to save a child. I can feel free to count myself among them after that day, because as that bear was running after me, my feet were moving so fast that it didn't seem humanly possible. I couldn't even feel them hitting the ground. As I breezed through that forest, I could have been flying and wouldn't even have known.

After a minute, Felicia's prediction had come true. The bear, too lethargic after his honey binge, was slowing down and giving up. The sight filled me with joyous relief. I even let out a mad cackle as I turned around to watch it slow down to a trot. I had done it. I had escaped. Now all I had to do was make it back to Samuel and Felicia without—

I didn't even get to finish my thought. As my head was turned the wrong way, I had been running straight toward a large jagged rock that was sticking up from the leaves and grass. I didn't even see it as my foot kicked hard into it, catching on its edge and sending me face-first into the dirt. All the wind burst out of me like a balloon, leaving me writhing on the ground in agony, half my face covered in dirt and pine needles, trying to suck in a full breath of air. As I rolled onto my hands and knees, I heard the fast, thundering footsteps of the bear as it closed the distance between us in a fraction of a second.

With a roar, the bear lunged at me, raising a paw that was as big as my skull and swiping it at me. Somehow, I was able to dive to the side and avoid it, but I wasn't going to give that woolly bear another chance to slash me to ribbons. With the air returning to my lungs, I scrambled to my feet faster than I ever had before and took off once more, sprinting for all it was worth. I didn't even have to look to know that the bear was still behind me. I could practically feel his hot breath on my heels.

"I'm coming!" I yelled, doing my best to warn my brother and sister. "I'm coming and he's right behind me! Get the honey! Get the honey!"

Ahead of me, I saw Samuel poke his head around the trunk of the tree. As soon as he saw me, his eyes opened up as wide as saucers and he jumped for the nearest branch, which happened to be the same one that Felicia was standing on. I could hear them arguing back and forth as I drew closer, but I couldn't make out what they were saying. When the bear and I were only a few yards away, the tree branch that held them gave out, sending them both tumbling to the ground. Immediately, they both leapt to their feet, waving their arms wildly around their heads as a massive cloud of honeybees swarmed out of the tree. The bees flooded out into the air, cascading from a hole in the trunk that had been created when the branch snapped off.

"Bees!" I hollered. I'm not sure why. Maybe it was the only thought that my brain could form at the moment. Felicia and Samuel were both well aware of the bees, seeing as they were valiantly fighting them already. Maybe my mind was just trying to warn me. If so, it didn't help. I ended up dashing straight into the thick swarm.

At once, I felt a sharp, burning pain on the right side of my neck, followed by another one on my left elbow. Behind me, I heard the bear baying in discomfort. It seemed he wasn't impervious to the insects after all. I couldn't believe how many of the little devils were flitting through the air. It was like they had a second reserve hive hidden in the trunk, like the first one was only a diversion. The sheer mass of the bees seemed to darken the sky itself, becoming so thick and loud that it obscured even the sun. The buzzing was an incredible sound, too. It was so powerful, so intense, it was all I could hear, like the entire sky was humming angrily along with them. As I heard Felicia yelp in pain from a sting, she turned back to Samuel and me.

"Run!" She screamed, abandoning the quest for the honey.

Samuel and I were on her heels in a heartbeat, swatting away as many of the tiny monsters as we could. I felt a couple of stings on the back on my neck as I ran. I couldn't believe it, but they were chasing us. The bees were intent on finishing us off. All I could do was wave my hands in the air like a maniac, doing my best to keep them from landing and stinging. It was making the run more difficult than usual, though. It seemed that with every couple of steps, there was a log or a rock or a thick bush just waiting to reach out and snatch my feet out from under me. Pebbles and acorns were like marbles under my shoes. Tall weeds became tripwires. At one point, I couldn't tell if I was moving ahead because I was running or if I was just in a constant state of stumbling forward, trying with all my might to stay on my feet. Either way, I was at least glad that the bear had stopped following me. I didn't see where it went, but hopefully it was the opposite direction of us.

I wasn't even sure we were going in the right direction. I could tell that we were going downhill, but the cloud of furious bees was still partially obstructing my view. The buzzing was still the only sound I could hear, other than the anguished cries of my siblings. After a minute, one that seemed to last for a thousand years, Felicia screamed out above the hum of the dreadful bees.

"I hear water!" she shouted.

How she heard it was beyond me, but she was right. After a few more steps, my own ears began to pick up the gentle rippling of a river, or at least a very large stream. Through a part in the bee cloud, I could see a ledge of a bluff up ahead, so I knew the water must have been directly below it. I also knew that we were going to have to jump. That fact didn't seem to faze Felicia or Samuel, so I wasn't going to let it affect me. We made it through one river. We'd make it through this one. The bees had made us desperate for a reprieve, and we knew the water below would hold it.

So . . . we jumped!

At the time, I didn't care that it made no sense for three children who couldn't swim to go hurling themselves into a river. Felicia and Samuel didn't care, either. They were both feeling the same way I was. I had already been stung more times than I could count and the thought of just one more was enough to push all of us over that ledge.

As it turned out, luck was on our side. The bluff couldn't have been more than twelve feet high, but it felt like a hundred as I was sailing through the air. My feet were still kicking as I dropped, like they were still trying to run even though the ground had ended. Also, although it was only twelve feet, I had never dropped from such a height. I had not been expecting the feeling of weightlessness, the one that made my heart feel like it was sliding up into my throat. I didn't care for it. Fortunately, it didn't last long.

All three of us crashed into the river with fervor. The water wasn't very deep, though, and I felt my knees smack against the bottom before I immediately pushed myself to the surface. The impact had hurt, but there was no serious damage. The throbbing bee stings were still the worst part. Beside me, Samuel and Felicia also resurfaced, gasping for breath and moaning in pain. Fortunately, this river was nearly as cold as the last one and it helped soothe the burning from the stings. As the water wasn't deep, we were able to stand up in it, letting the smooth current break around us as we tediously picked the stingers out of each other's flesh. Thankfully, none of us were allergic to bees. If we had been, there would have been nothing to do for it out here in the wilderness.

The sun was once again starting to lower toward the horizon as we dragged our sore, soggy carcasses out of the river, taking shelter underneath a large maple tree. I took a moment to look around, noticing that the landscape was much more level than it had been for the last day and a half.

"We should fill up the canteens while we're here," Felicia said, shaking the water from her hair just like a dog. "Don't know when we'll find water again."

Samuel searched the ground around his feet, his face wrinkled in confusion. After a moment, his head snapped back up to the bluff we had jumped off and he cursed loudly. "I don't believe it!" he shouted. "I left the pack up there!"

Felicia tensed up for several seconds, as if she were angry about it, and then deflated. "By the honey tree?" she asked dejectedly.

Samuel rubbed the back of his shaved head, flicking water droplets from his fingers. "Yup. The bees came out and I didn't think to grab it. Stupid!"

Felicia nodded, staring up at the green leaves above us. "Well . . . neither did I. Don't feel bad."

"I forgot all about it, too." I said, leaning against the trunk of the tree. It was the best I could do to ease Samuel's guilt. It was true, though. With the bear and the bees, we were all too focused on getting out of there alive. The pack just slipped all of our minds when we decided to run for it. We couldn't go back. We couldn't spare the time to scale the bluff or even try to find a way around. Even if we did, that pack was right next to a hive of ravenous honeybees and a bear that was likely still wandering around up there. The sugar, the blanket, the water canteens . . . all of it was gone for good.

Ignoring Samuel's muted swearing, I took stock of our surroundings, trying to see if I could locate anything that would tell us we were going in the right direction. From the look of it, we were on more foothills. We hadn't gone backward, but it seemed we had descended from the mountain faster than I'd ever expected.

"How long were we running for?" I asked, staring down at the trees and yellow wildflowers in the field across from us. "It looks like we made it over the mountain."

Samuel dropped down onto the grass in the shade, closing his eyes against the afternoon.

"Well, good. We're making great time, then. That means we can stay here for the night."

"I don't think so," Felicia countered, sounding more stern than usual. "We gotta keep moving and you know it."

"Come on," Samuel groaned. "I need to rest. After what we've just been through, I think we deserve it, don't you? And besides, my feet are starting to blister."

Felicia stood straight and stepped into the sun, stretching out her back and shielding her eyes with her hand as she squinted out at the field. At that moment, I couldn't help but notice that she looked so much older than thirteen. The shadows on her face, the tiny slivers of light through her fingers, they made it look like she had wrinkles, like she was thirty years older than she really was.

"We can rest when we're in Reading," she pressed, ringing the water from the hem of her shirt. "It looks like it's still gonna be a downhill walk for a while. No more climbing. It'll be easier. Come on."

Still lying on the ground, Samuel shook his head. "Nope. I'll go when my feet and these beestings stop throbbing."

"Get up, or me and Isaac will leave you behind."

"Will not."

"Will so!"

As the two of them argued, I heard a different sound coming from further up the river to our right. It was a familiar sound, but rather than being a comfort, it filled my insides with a dark dread.

"Felicia," I said over my shoulder, my eyes locked on the trees that were concealing the sound.

At the tone of my voice, Felicia and Samuel both stopped bickering and turned to me. "What is it?" Samuel asked, sounding worried.

I didn't say anything. I only let them listen for a moment before Felicia grabbed both of our hands, crushing my fingers in her inexplicably iron grip. "Come on!" She whispered angrily. "Back in the water! Get back in the water! Hurry!"

My first thought was to climb the tree and hide among the thick branches, but I followed her suggestion quickly and quietly, thankful that Samuel was doing the same thing. As the sound grew louder, we slipped back into the river and ducked low toward the middle where the water was deepest. We still had to crouch down on the bottom to get low enough, but only our heads were now poking out.

"They're still gonna see us!" Samuel whispered. I didn't want to say it, but I knew he was right.

At the last moment, before the group of men on horseback emerged from the trees, Felicia put her hand on top of my head and slowly pushed me under the surface. I barely had time to take in a breath of air before I slipped under, feeling the cold water rushing over my face. Beneath the current, I opened my eyes and could see the blurred image of Samuel with Felicia's other hand atop his head, holding him under with us. In front of us, the horses galloped right by. I could hear the hooves pounding into the dirt, sending vibrations through the water. As they rode past, the tremors became softer, and I had to take the chance to surface before my lungs decided to explode.

As gingerly as I could, I pushed myself up from the river bottom and poked my head above the ripples of the water, letting out my air and sucking in a breath as Felicia and Samuel bobbed up next to me. We stayed low in the small waves, careful not to make ourselves noticeable. We watched the three men ride until they were about twenty yards away, where they came to rest under a wide tree similar to the one we had just fled. They were all dressed in lengthy riding gear: leather chaps, heavy saddlebags, rifles, and I couldn't help but notice the length of rope on each of their saddles.

"Slave hunters?" Samuel whispered.

No one answered him, but we knew he was right. There was seemingly no other reason for the three men to be there. After Seth's warning back on the train, we knew it had to be true. As the men dismounted their horses and began gathering wood for a campfire, the tallest of them, the clear leader, turned to the side. Upon seeing his face, I had to stifle the mounting cry of horror that surfaced in the back of my throat.

Behind me, Felicia gasped. "Is that . . . ?"

"Sure is," Samuel said. He had seen it, too. There was really no mistaking that face, that hat, that military-like posture . . .

It was Mr. Slate.

Chapter 8

Mr. Cornelius Slate, not in a cotton field but still just as threatening, flexed his back and shoulders, staring out at the late afternoon sun. This was no good. This was no good at all. With him around, there was no way we could carry on. We would only hope to wait until he left before continuing.

"What is *he* doing here?" Samuel asked, keeping his voice quiet.

Felicia drew a deep breath and sighed. "Seems to me like he's out here searching for three runaway slaves."

"You mean us," I said morosely.

"I do," she replied.

Samuel groaned. "What do we do now?"

The soft babbling of the water was the only response. For a long minute, we simply remained there, up to our chins in the river water, watching Slate and his men spark up a fire and begin cooking something that smelled an awful lot like pork. That was the worst torture, I think. They were relaxing, laughing, and eating delicious food as the sun started to set. All we could do was sit in the cold water, getting soggy and cold, shivering and smelling food we couldn't have.

Finally, after several hours, the sun had all but set behind the horizon, casting mesmerizing tendrils of pink and purple across the day's lingering moments. From behind me, Felicia tapped me on the shoulder.

"We need to get out of this water," she said, her voice frail and concerned.

I only nodded in agreement, all too eager to escape the frigid confines of the river.

"Sure do," Samuel agreed.

With our teeth chattering, we did our best to stand straight and slink quietly out of the water, taking care to not disturb the surface too much. We moved slowly and steadily up toward the bank. If one of us slipped and fell now . . . that would be the end. Thankfully, we were able to stay upright and crawl stealthily onto the muddy grass. The three of us were sopping wet as we huddled underneath our tree, still in view of Slate and his men. The sight of their fire and the smell of their food were unbelievably alluring, I couldn't deny. The only thing we could do now was wedge ourselves together and hope that our shared body heat could prevent us from freezing. Mercifully, it was slowly working.

Over the next couple of hours, the three of us just sat together, not talking, not making a sound, and napping in shifts to ensure that none of us would snore. As long as we stayed out of sight and out of earshot of Mr. Slate and his men, we were in good shape. After a while, our clothes even began to dry a bit. Yet again, it was Samuel who finally demanded a course of action.

"What are we gonna do?" he whispered. "We can't keep going. It looks to me like they know exactly where we're going *and* how we're gettin' there."

Felicia considered this for a moment, her eyes locked on the trio of men just beyond us. I looked over at her, trying to figure just what was happening in her mind, but I just couldn't tell. It wasn't something I was used to.

Pressing the issue, Samuel went on. "We ain't never gonna make it to that train this way. We need to go back and find another route North."

"We will so make it to that train," I said defiantly. Since Felicia was remaining silent, I felt the need to defend our current journey.

Samuel rounded on me. "Oh? Whaddya wanna bet that's where Slate and his goons are headed? 'Cause I'd bet that's exactly where!"

I opened my mouth to reply, but no words came out. Instead, my eyes darted through the grass around me, as if hoping to find a proper argument there.

"Yeah, you know I'm right," Samuel said gravely, preemptively trumping any comeback I might have found.

Beside me, Felicia decided to finally speak up. "We're making it to that train," she whispered confidently. "Not only that, but we're gonna get there early."

Samuel let out a breathy laugh. "Well, I gotta hear how you plan on doing that."

"Easy," she replied, pointing over to Slate's campfire. "They're asleep."

My head spun around slowly and I fixed my gaze on Slate's dying campfire. I couldn't hear snoring or anything, but they were definitely motionless, something that suggested she was right.

"I've been watching them," Felicia explained. "They ain't moved in a while. None of 'em. They're all asleep."

Samuel sighed. "Even if they are, what's that got to do with anything?"

"We're gonna take their horses," Felicia said plainly, as if it she were suggesting no more than a leisurely stroll.

Samuel laughed quietly. "I'm sorry," he said. "I think I had something plumb crazy in my ear. It sounded like you said we were gonna steal Mr. Slate's horses."

Felicia nodded. "Yep. Three horses, three of us. We all know how to ride."

I couldn't help but think her idea was a good one. She was right. We all knew how to handle a horse. During the early months of the year, the field workers were sowing seeds and plowing the fields to make sure that the season's crop would come in nice and thick. Plowing required horses. We sometimes used oxen and mules, but horses were just as necessary. Besides, they were just plain smarter. Because of this, we all knew how to saddle a mount. Often, children would ride atop the mule or the horse, helping to control it and make the process much faster. I always enjoyed it because it required less work. Also, I liked being around the animals.

"Are you serious?" I asked.

Felicia nodded again. "Dead serious. Look, they didn't even take the saddles off. Poor horsies. All we gotta do is hop on and take off."

"No way," Samuel argued. "Soon as we go up there, those horses are gonna spook and then Mr. Slate wakes up and catches us. That's how your plan ends."

"I don't think we'd spook them," I said absentmindedly, unsure of which side of the argument I wanted to take. "They've all been around us plenty. We ain't really strangers to 'em."

Samuel put his face in the palm of his hands. "You both gone nuts," he said with a large sigh. "All right. Fine. Let's do it. But, when we're hanging by our necks from that tree, you remember that I tried to talk you out of it."

Felicia nodded. "Noted. Now, come on. Very quiet. When we get up to 'em, make sure to take a second and get friendly with those horses before you mount up."

"Sure," Samuel said sarcastically. "Make friends."

Felicia and I ignored him. Gathering our courage, we waited for the adrenaline to surge its way through our chilled bodies before we took our first steps forward. In the night, we were all but invisible. With our dark clothes and skin, we were nearly undetectable. It only took a few seconds for us to slink over to the edge of Slate's camp, the sound of our footsteps camouflaged by the crackling of their fire. In just a few more moments, we were sidling up to the horses, cooing quietly and making slow movements to keep from frightening them. Samuel unbound their reins from the tree before he and I took the Mustangs, both of them dark with patches of lighter colors splashed randomly across their bodies. Felicia, on the other hand, was stroking the head of Slate's snow-white female thoroughbred. I couldn't help but smile, thinking of Slate's reaction when he saw that his prize mare had been taken.

From under the horse's neck, Felicia gave me a nod, which I took to be the signal to hop into the saddle. I kept it as quiet as I could, but the leather saddle creaked a bit as I hoisted myself up. The horse beneath me grumbled softly, as did the white one as Felicia pulled herself onto its back. I looked over to find Samuel, but he wasn't there. In a moment of panic, I imagined the worst, that Slate had caught him. Whipping around the other way, I saw that all three hunters were still sleeping soundly.

"Psst!" someone whispered. I once again whirled my head around to Samuel's horse. This time, he was there in the saddle, grinning widely as he held up three pairs of dirty riding boots, the laces clutched in his fist. Felicia and I had to suppress our giggles. Now, Slate and his men would have no horses and no shoes to protect their feet from the rough, rocky terrain when they woke up.

As gingerly as we could, we nudged the horses forward, keeping the pace very slow. The soft grass kept their hooves muffled, which enabled us to slip away without disturbing Slate at all. As we got a bit further form the faint glow of the fire, we gave the steeds a heel and put them at a bit of a gallop. Riding at night wasn't the best idea, especially on unfamiliar terrain, so we would be sure to stop soon. We just needed to put plenty of distance between us and those hunters beforehand. Once we got far enough away, we finally burst out laughing, exhilarated that our daring heist had gone off without a hitch. In the horse saddlebags, we found plenty of food and water to last us for the rest of our journey. We were still damp from the river, but our high spirits made us feel invincible. In the moonlight, we rode and laughed and sang and cheered. For one night, we were full of hope. For one night, we believed we were going to be free.

For one night.

*** *** ***

The next morning was an early one. We had stopped after about ten miles or so, to sleep. We knew that even if Slate and his boys had awakened, they couldn't track us in the dark, so a few miles were practically a million. We ate their food, drank their water, and used their saddle blankets to sleep on. Even though we only got a few hours' rest, we were feeling better than ever as we set off again in the crisp morning air. Our spirits were high, our bellies were full, and we were feeling hopeful that we would be in Chesterfield before long. We just needed our luck to hold out.

On horseback, the foothills were passing underneath us in record time. Hills and rocks and trees all passed by without a second thought as we laughed and joked our way across the countryside. The journey seemed almost enjoyable this way. For those few hours, we forgot about all the things we'd lost, all the trouble we'd been in, all the pain we were still in, we simply enjoyed the freedom of it. We enjoyed each other's company. If this was anything like our new lives in the North would be, we knew we'd enjoy every day of it.

As the ground beneath us began to level out once again, we knew we must have been approaching the valley on the other side of the mountain. It was here, as the sun was at mid-morning, that Samuel finally decided to drop the three large pairs of boots that he'd stolen from Slate and his men. We had all tried them on, just to make sure we couldn't use them, but they had been much too large for our feet. As the boots dropped to the grass with a heavy thud, Samuel let out a raucous laugh and then sighed, his eyes squinting as if he were thinking of something.

"What is it?" I asked him, curious as to what could so suddenly rob him of his merriment.

He looked over at me and adjusted himself in the saddle. "I was just wonderin'," he said, staring into the distance. "You think they'll be all right? Stuck out there with no horses and no supplies?"

I smiled and nodded. "Yeah. I think they'll manage."

"We did," Felicia chimed in, smiling over at us. "And we're just kids. They're grown men."

Samuel considered this with a goofy grin on his face. "Hmmm. Yeah, we didn't do too bad, did we?"

"Sure didn't," Felicia replied.

The three of us rode on in silence for a moment until Samuel chimed in with another thought. "I like to imagine Mr. Slate's face when he saw his horses were gone. I bet he was so steamed!"

I laughed loudly. "I bet that frown of his was somethin' to behold!"

"Ugh!" Felicia groaned. "I will never miss that ugly frown of his. Glad I'll never see it again!"

"No question!" I agreed with a grin, scratching leaves out of my thick hair. With as long as it was getting, I was picking up all kinds of leaves and twigs and dirt every time I laid my head down to rest. I suddenly wanted to shave it all off like Samuel's.

"You know," Samuel said, staring into the distance again. "Lookin' back . . . I don't reckon I've ever seen old Slate crack a smile. Not once."

I searched my memory, thinking there must have been at least one occasion that Slate had let the frown falter. To my surprise, though, I couldn't recall a single one. "Wow," I said. "Me neither."

"Nobody taught him how to be happy," Felicia joked.

I chuckled. "Yeah, I guess his Ma and Pa didn't hug him enough as a youngster. That must be it."

"Actually, that ain't what I heard," Felicia said, yawning loudly as Samuel and I turned to her. "I heard his Ma and Pa weren't never around and he was raised by his house maid . . . who was a slave. Just like us."

Samuel snorted. "Raised by a slave and still came out evil? Can't be!"

"I hear it's true!" Felicia went on. "I hear she took care of him and cooked for him and cleaned for him like he was one of her own. I reckon she was more of a mama to him than anyone."

"Where'd you hear that craziness?" I asked, genuinely curious.

Without looking back, Felicia just shrugged. "I dunno. Just heard it around. You know how things are."

I looked over at Samuel and he rolled his eyes. I had never heard one bit of the story Felicia was spouting. I wondered who had told it to her. As we came upon the downward crest of the final foothill, though, the thought was pushed completely from my mind by what I was seeing.

"Holy smokes," Samuel breathed, voicing what Felicia and I were both thinking.

There, maybe a hundred yards down below us, was the valley that signified we had fully crossed over the mountain. The base of the hill ended in a magnificent, lush, green meadow. It was enormous, framed in the distance by forest and accompanied by a small stream that filtered down the hillside and culminated in a huge, crystal-clear pond to the right. From where we were sitting, the view was breathtaking. We still couldn't see the town that Seth had told us about, but we no longer doubted it was there. We were more determined than ever. As we perched there, looking down at such a beautiful slice of the earth, we could feel that it was within reach, that we were going to make it all the way and nothing was going to stop us. We spent a few minutes there, taking in the sight. None of us were eager to let it go. After all, we had never seen such amazing views. A good view on the plantation was just seeing your bed after Slate let everybody come in. Compared to that, this seemed like another planet altogether.

"That's something, ain't it?" I asked, trying to soak it all into my eyeballs.

Felicia nodded. "Sure is."

As we sat there, the tranquil silence of nature began to turn into a faint rumble. It was soft to begin with, but grew louder and louder with each passing second. At first, I couldn't even be sure I was really hearing it. Before long, though, the rumbling grew and grew, becoming frighteningly loud and strong enough to vibrate the ground under us. It was powerful enough that we could feel it through our horses. The first thing that crossed my mind was thunder, but I had never heard it roll for so long.

"What is that?!" Samuel asked, pulling tight on his reins to keep his horse in place. "Is that an earthquake?"

"No!" Felicia said, her eyes wide. "Look!" Over the head of her agitated steed, she pointed down to the valley below, where an enormous herd of wild horses appeared from around the length of the hill.

Led by a large, jet-black Mustang, the herd swept across the meadow, following the contours of the grass and weeds. Despite the sound of their feet thundering underneath them, they moved so gracefully together, like they were carried by the wind itself. Maybe they *were* the wind. They were certainly moving fast enough to be. There were so many colors and patterns, spots of white and splotches of brown and pale yellow, but they all blended together so perfectly that the herd seemed like one massive creature, a living wave of wildness and freedom and untamed power. I had never seen anything so wondrous in my life. Like Samuel, though, I was suddenly having trouble keeping my horse from moving.

I leaned back in the saddle and pulled the reins hard. "Whoa!" I croaked out. "Easy, boy!"

Even Felicia was having difficulties. She was pulling back for all she was worth, but her white mare was chomping at the bit in her mouth.

"What's gotten into them?" Samuel asked, grabbing a fistful of mane.

Felicia's eyes flitted from our horses to the wild group below and she suddenly gave a tiny smile. "I think the same thing that's gotten into us," she replied.

Samuel looked down at the wild ponies, which had all slowed down to crowd around and take a drink from the pond on the right. "Yeah . . . I think so, too."

"You thinking what I'm thinking?" Felicia asked, looking over at Samuel.

He drew in a huge breath and let it out in a huff. "Yep. I believe I am."

"It's now or never," Felicia said, her pearly teeth gleaming in the morning sun.

My eyes darted back and forth between them. "To do what?" I asked, oblivious as to what they were scheming.

Samuel gave a long, drawn out sigh. "Welp! We been walkin' our whole lives, so . . . it ain't nothin' new."

Together, Felicia and Samuel hoisted their legs over their saddles and stepped down onto the ground, their hands prying at the buckles underneath the bellies of their horses. If I hadn't known better, I would have guessed that they were taking the saddles off of their steeds.

"What are you doing?" I asked, looking over at Felicia. "What happened to getting there early?"

"Just get down and take off that saddle," Felicia instructed. "Pull everything off. Packs, blankets, all of it."

"Are you crazy?" I protested. "After what we went through to *get* these?"

"Don't be a baby!" Samuel shouted from my left, pulling the heavy leather saddle from his impatient Mustang.

On my right, Felicia was stripping off the blanket and tossing it to the ground, leaving Slate's horse totally bare and blindingly white. With a pouting grimace, I grudgingly stepped down from my own mount and began peeling the belts loose, loosening the leather straps until I was able to slide the saddle off and let it crash to the ground. To their credit, the horses were still holding their place, though they were stamping their hooves and snorting loudly all the while. I don't know how I could've been so dense, but it finally dawned on me what we were doing.

I suppose there are different types of slavery in this world. Plenty of different types. You don't have to be a man or a woman or a child—or even human—to want to be free. Everyone and every living thing has the desire to live their life the way they want. To be ourselves, without anyone else's permission, is something all of us want. To force someone or something to do otherwise is just cruel, no matter if it's man or beast. Just like us, those horses had smelled the scent of freedom and they were captured by it. As good as it was to have them, the three of us were not cruel enough to deny it to them.

Felicia gave the thoroughbred a smack on the hindquarters and she bolted forward with a high-pitched whinny. The other two didn't even need a word. They fell in immediately behind her, tearing down the hill at a blinding speed. I couldn't help but smile as they thrashed their heads and kicked their legs, seized by the beautiful exultation of the moment. Within seconds, they were mingling with the crowd of wild horses below, sipping from the pond and making new friends. After just a couple of minutes, the muscle-bound black Mustang reared up on his hind legs and took off once more, waiting for the rest of the herd to follow well in order. The three of us watched in silence as the last of the animals disappeared around the other side of the meadow. In just a few seconds, the rumbling of their hooves couldn't even be heard.

"I reckon they'll be fine, now," Samuel said, a satisfied grin on his face.

"Yeah," I agreed, feeling moisture building in my eyes. "They're where they belong."

Behind us, Felicia was pulling a full saddlebag off the ground and hoisting it over her shoulder. "Well, the food's all gone," she said. "But, grab what you can. Water skins, blankets, whatever you can carry. Leave the rest."

Groaning, Samuel and I began gathering what few supplies we could manage. Now that we were on foot again, things would be considerably more difficult. Sadly, I had no idea just how difficult.

***   ***   ***

Not long after we set the horses free, the three of us had barreled into the forest that we had seen from the hilltop. We weren't fond of having to soldier through more dense wilderness, but this forest was a bit more traveled than the one we'd come from the day before. There were paths in these woods. Nothing especially clear and tamed, but definite paths, for sure. It was a sign that people frequented this area, which was both good and bad. Good, because it meant we were getting close to civilization, Bad, though, because we never knew who might be walking through at any given time. For this reason alone, we made sure to stay near the paths . . . but never on them. We needed to be able to duck into thicker brush if we encountered someone. We needed to be able to hide from any possible dangers. It was a good thing we had formulated this plan, because danger was exactly what was waiting for us.

It was still morning, or so the sun led me to believe, and we had stumbled upon a large patch of blackberry bushes hidden just off one of the paths we were following. It was a welcome sight for us, as we hadn't had anything to eat since the night before, and we were all feeling a bit of a rumble in our stomachs. For a long while, we stood there, picking our way through the bushes, snatching handfuls of the deliciously sweet and tangy berries. Without any kind of collection pail, we simply ate them right off the vine, careful of the painful thorns that were waiting. After just a few minutes, our fingers were stained purple and red with the berry juice and blood droplets from angry thorns. We didn't mind a few finger pricks if it meant we could dine on the delicious fruit they guarded. As we continued eating in silence, we were able to hear the voices of the slave hunters before they were upon us.

"Which way did he go?" a voice asked. It was male, young, and was clearly excited about something.

"I don't know!" an older man replied. "Split up and keep looking! He's gotta be around here somewhere! You go East. Me and Hank will go West a bit and try to head him off!"

Beside me, Felicia's head was already swiveling from side to side. "Hunters!" she whispered urgently. "Get down! Where's Samuel?"

Samuel, who had wandered away from us to pluck berries from his own bush, was nowhere to be found. I barely had time to look for him, however, before rapid footsteps could be heard on the path ahead of us. Somebody was running full tilt in my direction.

"Down!" Felicia hissed, grasping the sleeve of my filthy shirt and yanking me down to the ground. From where we were, we were easily able to shimmy in between the low, thick branches of the bush and hide beneath its leafy cover. Also, we were able to see the path clearly from the ground, which meant we got a good eyeful when a young, slender, panic-stricken slave came running down the thin dirt path toward us. His ragged clothes and terrified facial expression were enough to tell me that this was the runaway that the slave hunters were currently chasing. As he looked back over his shoulder to try and spot his pursuers, his bare foot slid on a handful of moist leaves and he slammed hard into the ground, rolling to a stop right in front of where Felicia and I huddled in the blackberry bush.

For a split second, as the dust from his fall was still hanging in the air, the young man's eyes met mine, and we shared a brief look of hysterical fear before he got to his feet. In that moment, that split second that felt like a whole year, it seemed that he and I had come to an understanding. He knew that we were going to stay hidden, that we wouldn't risk capture to aid him, and as the hunters approached on horseback, we knew that this was probably the last meaningful contact he was going to have before his death. For a moment, I was afraid he would suddenly reach into the prickly bush and pull me out of it, leaving me as bait for the hunters while he got away. Fortunately, he was a better man that that. He got up without a word and sprinted onward down the path. Felicia and I watched him go for a few seconds, only to see another figure appear from nowhere and hit him from the side with a vicious tackle, knocking both of them into the depths of a thick berry bush on the side of the path. I had only seen the second figure for an instant, for a fraction of a second, but I knew it had been Samuel. He had been the one tackling the runaway.

Moments later, two scruffy, pale-skinned men with rifles in hand galloped right past where we hid, their steeds kicking dirt in our faces as they passed. "Come on, Hank!" one of them shouted. "We need this one!"

After several painfully long seconds, the men had ridden far enough away that we could no longer hear the hoof beats of their horses. Immediately, Felicia and I clamored out of our cover and dashed over to where Samuel and the runaway had landed. It was no wonder that the hunters hadn't seen them. They had landed in the center of a large bush and had disappeared beneath the branches just like jumping into a pile of autumn leaves. The thick leaves and thorns had swallowed them up completely, making them virtually invisible to a passerby.

"I'm Samuel," we heard him say from beneath the berries.

"The name's Mavin Joseph," the runaway replied. "But, everybody calls me JoJo. Don't ask me why. They just do."

"Are you two all right?" Felicia asked the bush, trying to carefully pry apart the mangled branches.

"Here," Samuel said, sticking his hand out of the greenery. Felicia and I grabbed a hold of it and heaved, slowly dragging him out of the bush. His other hand was clasped in JoJo's, helping him out of the thorns with the same action. It took a minute to fully untangle their clothing from the branches, and both of them were bleeding lightly in several places, but they seemed fine otherwise. I would think a few angry red scratches were a small price to pay to have your life still intact.

It was then that I noticed JoJo eyeing Felicia and me suspiciously, like he wasn't quite sure who we were. Luckily, Samuel picked up on it and cleared his throat to break the uneasy tension. "JoJo, this is my sister Felicia," he said, gesturing to her. JoJo gave her a polite nod. "And this is my little brother Isaac."

JoJo nodded again. "Yeah, I saw 'em hiding in them bushes like a couple of scared rats," he said, an acidic tone to his voice. I was about to reply in kind when he seemed to correct himself.

"You was right to hide, though," he said, nervously wiping his hands on his pants. "If they'd seen you, you woulda been taken. Or killed. It don't really matter to them. They get paid either way."

"We know. We ran into a few just yesterday," Felicia said to him.

"Where you headed?" Samuel asked, popping a berry into his mouth.

JoJo shrugged his lean shoulders and looked in both directions, still clearly nervous about being a wanted man. "Don't really know," he said. "Anywhere's better than here, I think."

Samuel raised his eyebrows and cast a questioning look over at Felicia and me. I couldn't tell what he was thinking, though, until he opened his mouth to speak. "You want to go with us?" he asked.

JoJo suddenly looked down at Samuel. "Where *you* goin'?"

Felicia raised her hand and pointed in the direction that we had been walking all morning. "There's a town just a couple days' walk that way. It's called Chesterfield. There's a train that stops there, a train that can carry us North to a place where we can all be safe—for good!"

JoJo bit his lower lip as he pondered the suggestion. After a moment, though, he simply shook his head. "Nah. I appreciate what you done for me," he said to Samuel, "But I think I'm better off on my own. We'd best get movin', now. There's slave hunters all around these parts. You three be careful."

With a final nod, JoJo turned and made to break into a run once more, but Samuel spoke before he could tale his first step. "JoJo," he said, sticking out his hand. "Good Luck, my friend."

With the first hint of a smile I'd seen from him, JoJo grasped Samuel's hand and gave it a solid shake. "You too, youngster." He released Samuel's hand, threw a wink at Felicia and me, and then instantly took off at a dead sprint, disappearing from view as the forest swallowed him up.

With a sigh, I stepped up beside Samuel and propped my elbow upon his shoulder. "You think he'll make it?" I asked, smiling at the place in the trees where JoJo had vanished.

There was an odd silence that came over Samuel as he stared after his new friend. I didn't understand why, but I took my arm off of my brother and stood straight. "He'll be fine," I said, awkwardly, trying to break the unfamiliar stillness. "Don't ya think?"

"No," Samuel replied quietly. "I don't." Without looking at me, he tossed another blackberry into his mouth and turned to walk away, plucking randomly at the bushes as he moped down the path.

Felicia and I exchanged a confused glance, but we followed after him without a word. Samuel had a habit of being serious, even when it was unnecessary, but this was still out of character for him. I had been noticing all sorts of things about my siblings that had seemed odd since our journey began. They were being changed by the trip, molded by the unseen hand of fate. As we walked in silence next to the path that had just held slave hunters, I couldn't help but wonder why I was the only one who hadn't been changed by our trials. Maybe I was just being biased, but I couldn't see one way that the journey had altered me. In such a short period of time, Felicia had become so much more mature, so much wiser. Samuel had become so much stronger, more assertive. What had I become? I couldn't say. The fact that I had no answer was upsetting to me.

The rest of the day passed uneventfully, which we were glad of. We made good progress, but we were moving slower than usual. The high that we had been riding the day before had seeped out of us. In addition to this, several days without proper nutrition and rest were taking their toll on us. Our muscles ached all over, the straps from our packs were bruising our shoulders from the constant pressure, and we had to stop a few times when one of us was feeling lightheaded and dizzy. None of us said it, but we all knew the truth: We weren't going to last much longer. We needed to get on that train—fast!

That night, we spread our packs and saddle blankets beneath the twilit sky, making sure that we were well off any path in the forest. We hadn't spoken to each other much since JoJo left us and it didn't seem like that was going to change. None of us were really in the mood for conversation. The sounds of the forest grew louder as we settled down to sleep. The sounds of our stomachs growling, however, were the only ones that seemed to bother us.

"Boy," Samuel said, adjusting his pack as a makeshift pillow. "Them blackberries don't last long, do they?"

Felicia yawned and rubbed her face. "Sure don't."

"Yeah," I agreed. "I'm so hungry."

"Just try not to think about it," Felicia said, rolling onto her side with a soft groan. "Get some sleep. Can't be hungry if you're asleep."

I pulled my blanket tightly around my sore body and sighed. "Yeah." At that moment, my belly let out a mighty rumble, sounding like thunder was rolling in my gut.

"Quit that," Samuel said. "It's making mine act up."

"Well, I can't really stop it, can I?" I retorted.

Neither of them argued. We didn't even have the strength to argue. We could only lie there after an exhausting day and let our eyelids grow heavy. That, and listen to our stomachs gurgle loudly in the darkness. In no time at all, sleep was pulling me under, where I dreamed of running across a wide open field. I don't know what I was running to or from, only that I was running as fast as I could, but it never seemed to be fast enough.

The next morning came with less of a chill, but with a breeze that was strong enough to whistle across your ears and prevent you from sleeping. Eventually, it pushed us all out of our slumber and prodded us to continue. Reluctantly, we obeyed, knowing that we had no other choice.

As we packed up our meager belongings, Samuel groaned loudly, startling Felicia and me. "We have *got* to find some food," he said forcefully. "Real food."

Felicia sighed and finished packing her bag. "I know, Samuel, but . . . it ain't like there's a banquet hall around here. We don't know how to trap or hunt, we don't have anything to cook, and the only thing we know for sure that ain't poisonous are the berries."

"Yeah, and we didn't pick any to save for later," Samuel grumbled, kicking a loose twig on the ground.

"No," Felicia relented. "No, we didn't. We have to keep going, though. There's nothing else we can do."

I was barely listening to them as I gathered my blanket and empty water canteen. My thoughts had wandered back to the cabin that we had called home until a few days ago. It was odd that it seemed like an entire lifetime ago. Mornings were some of the best times we had as a family. Pa would joke with us, wrestle us out of bed and pretend that we were strong enough to beat him. Ma would somehow make a delicious meal out of nothing more than some beans and hardtack, something that seemed impossible to us. What I wouldn't give to have one of those meals right now.

"Wait," I said, suddenly remembering something. "What did Ma say . . . that night before we got on the train?"

Felicia and Samuel stopped talking and turned toward me, their eyebrows pulled together in confusion.

"She said to just ask her," I said. "Didn't she?"

Felicia nodded, smiling as her eyes stared into the distance. "She told me to tell it to the wind," she said, lifting her hand so that the morning breeze could weave its way through her fingers. "And she'd hear me."

"Well," Samuel said, rubbing the back of his head. "Go ahead and give it a shot. I'm starving. We could use all the help we can get."

Felicia nodded. "Okay." With her arms held out to her sides, she leaned her head back and closed her eyes, letting the wind wrap her up like an invisible cloak. She drew in a deep breath and then let it out slowly. "Mama," she said softly. "Mama, if you can hear me . . . we need food. Please . . . tell us what to do. Tell us where to go. Please, Ma."

I hadn't realized it at first, but Samuel and I had frozen in place, unwilling to move in case the words would somehow be disturbed on their path home. Despite the absurdity of the notion, we were all listening, straining our ears to the wind as if our mother's voice would actually carry all the way to where we were. I can't deny that a part of me was hoping it would. I wanted to believe that she could still be with us, even from so far away. After several minutes of careful, attentive listening, we gradually began to move again, glumly accepting that it wasn't going to happen. As we were preparing to leave, however, something did catch the attention of Felicia.

She raised her head and sniffed the air. "You smell that? Smell the breeze," Felicia said, her eyes suddenly wide. Instantly, our noses lifted into the air like a pack of bloodhounds searching for the scent of wild game.

Samuel then stood on his toes, sniffing long breaths of air as he made his way over to her. "Smells like smoke," he said.

I didn't even have time to step over to them before the smell invaded my nostrils, bringing me to life from the inside out. "Someone's cooking!" I exclaimed.

Felicia wasted no time. She slung her pack over her shoulder and scuttled off in the direction of the smell, barely bothering to step over fallen logs and other debris from the forest. Samuel and I immediately went after her. The smell was luring us like moths to a lamplight. We were so hungry, we were caught in its pull and there was no turning back. We had to see what was cooking.

I'm not sure how long we walked, but by the time we had cleared the tree line, the morning dew had burned off the fallen leaves. The sun was higher now, shining down from a steeper angle, and we were able to see the source of the enticing smell that had dragged us through the woods in the wrong direction.

"Well, I guess it makes sense," Felicia said, ushering us back until we were camouflaged by the trees. "JoJo had to come from somewhere."

Just down the hill from us, a large rectangular plantation house sat serenely in a flat, green acre. Slaves were busy outside and in, gardening, trimming hedges, collecting lawn clippings, even pruning flowers. The white house stood out remarkably against the lush backdrop of the forest and the grass. In the backyard, a lengthy line of laundry was billowing gently in the breeze, the sheets and aprons appearing to dance like ghosts in the air. Above it all, a thin, wispy trail of pale smoke stretched into the blue sky, still smelling of delicious cooked food. As much as I didn't enjoy seeing another slave plantation, I couldn't help but appreciate the view. It would have been beautiful, like a place I would like to live, if not for the dozens of Confederate soldiers who were filtering in and out of the building.

Upon seeing the grey coats, the three of us threw down our packs and immediately dropped to our bellies on the grass, hiding ourselves as best we could.

"What next!?" Samuel asked in frustration, clutching grass in his fists. "What else can go wrong?"

"They got food in there!" Felicia said, her eyes fixed on the big old house.

I turned to look at her. "Yeah, but they also got a whole mess of soldiers with guns. You did see them, didn't you?"

"Sure did," Felicia replied. "I heard that whenever a bunch of soldiers comes across a house, they can take it over. They can stay there and eat the food and do whatever they want to."

"Why wouldn't they?" Samuel asked, shielding his face from the morning sun. "Sure beats sleeping on the ground."

"And starving in the woods," I added.

"We gotta get in there," Felicia whispered, literally licking her lips as she watched the house.

I turned my head and squinted my fuzzy eyes down toward the plantation, trying to find what she was staring at. It took a second, but I was able to spot a relatively young slave woman wearing a pale blue frock with her dark hair tied back in a red bandana. As my eyes fell upon her, she was coming out of the back of the house and approaching some laundry that was hanging on a line. She took a few of the sheets in her hands, caressing them with her fingers before frowning and letting them go. They must still be too wet to take in.

Beside me, Felicia let out a sly chuckle. "I'm going in," she said.

Samuel sighed loudly. "Assuming you are stupid enough to think that's a good idea, how exactly would you suggest you do it?"

Felicia pushed herself up from the grass and got her feet underneath her. She stayed hunkered down, but she was clearly ready to run. "You know how it is to be a slave," she said, keeping her eyes on the laundry. "You're nothin' to the master, whoever that is. They don't even want to think about you. They just want you to do your job and don't mess nothin' up. If you're doing everything right, nobody notices you at all. You're invisible. Them soldiers ain't been here long enough to know every name and face of every worker in that house. They ain't even gonna notice me."

Samuel and I exchanged a glance. We wanted to argue with her, but her point was completely valid. She was absolutely right. The best you could hope for as a slave was to do your job well enough to be left alone. In general, the master wouldn't want to have to bother with you. So if you didn't mess up and you kept your eyes down, you could get by without anyone even taking note of you.

Felicia grinned over at our dumbfounded faces. "Now who's stupid?" she asked jovially. "Wish me luck."

"Wait!" Samuel hissed. "You crazy?"

"You wanna eat, don't you?" she retorted. "Don't worry, I got me a plan."

Before Samuel or I could say anything else, she was off, sprinting fast down the hill as if she were well rested and fresh as a daisy. I don't think I'd ever seen her move so gracefully, with such purpose. She made it to the laundry line in just a few seconds flat and no one seemed to notice at all.

Using the clothes themselves as cover, she hid within them until she found something to pull down and slip over her head. As she made her way to the back door of the house, I saw that it had been an apron. She was now dressed as a house worker. She certainly looked the part, but I still had to hope and pray that no one found her out. As she slipped into the house itself, I could only hold my breath and wait.

Chapter 9

Felicia stepped into the enormous house and flattened herself against the nearest wall, taking stock of her surroundings. She knew she needed to look like she belonged here. Bumping into walls or knocking things over was a sure way to get her caught. She took a moment to slow her breathing and still her trembling hands. The adrenaline in her veins was wreaking havoc on her. If she was going to blend in, she needed to seem natural, like she had spent a thousand mornings doing the same work. As she wiped her sweating palms on the front of her still-damp apron, she felt a lump in one of the pockets. As she stuck her hand in to retrieve it, she saw that it was a wash rag. As two very tall, very stern Confederate troops marched by her, she turned to her right and immediately began rubbing the cloth on the side of a wooden bookshelf. To her relief, her ruse worked. The men strolled right by without a second glance.

Felicia decided to stick to this strategy. If she was just an innocent house girl dusting the shelves and baseboards, no one would care enough to even look at her. Then, she could sneak away with her pockets stuffed with food. It was as good a plan as any.

The house was full of interesting smells. There was the food, of course, but there was also the rich smell of the wood that the house was made of. It smelled much like the forest that she and her brothers had just come from. Intermingled with it were the scents of pipe tobacco, sod, and the unpleasant twinge of body odor. With so many men cramming themselves into the house, it was unavoidable.

Felicia soon discovered that she was in a dining area. In front of her to the left, behind a large pillar of pine and under a candlelit chandelier made of deer antlers, a lengthy table was laden with delicious food and drink. A handful of soldiers, some in full uniform, some just in trousers, sat around the table, their hands and mouths full of eggs, bacon, and fluffy pan fritters. They joked and laughed with each other, completely oblivious of the girl that had come from nowhere. Vaguely, Felicia found herself wondering who the house belonged to. Who were the owners of this plantation, of the lovely home that these soldiers had commandeered? Where were they? Were they aware that the Confederates were eating all their food and using the slaves for their own needs? Or had there been a choice at all? It didn't matter, really. Felicia knew she had more important things to worry about.

As she slipped through the nearest door, she found herself in a long hallway that passed behind the dining room and ran the length of the house. She turned to the right, following her nose and the intoxicating fragrance of frying meat. As she continued to feign dusting, she passed a door on the right, one that was partially closed, but had an urgent murmur of voices inside it. She paused outside the jamb, making sure they weren't paying any attention to the hallway.

"I'm telling you not to worry, sir," said one of the voices. "The men *will* be in place, and once they are, we will attack from here and here."

Immediately, Felicia was intrigued by this conversation. She swallowed her trepidation and peeked the side of her head around the edge of the open door, using just one eye to take in the sight.

The room was some sort of study. There was an ornately-carved wooden desk that rested atop a thick, brown rug. A tall arching window in front of it allowed the early sun to spill through, illuminating the extensive collection of books on the far wall, as well as the men who were huddled around the desk.

They were all Confederate soldiers, middle-aged by the looks of them. The one behind the desk, sitting with his hands folded in front of him, sported a thick, white beard from the bottom of his chin. His heavy eyebrows were furrowed tightly as he grimaced down at a map in front of him. Beside him, a taller, red-haired man was pointing vehemently at the map as he spoke, his bony finger knocking loudly on the desk's wooden surface. In front of the desk, sitting lazily in a chair, a portly fellow with a ridiculously wide mustache rested his head on his fist as the other two argued. He seemed to be fighting the powerful urge to fall asleep.

The man behind the desk gestured to the sleepy one. "Captain Keeper here has informed me that we are running out of supplies, that we are low on gunpowder, food, even things as simple as fresh socks. So, tell me, Colonel . . . when we engage the enemy, do you plan on charging them with nothing but bayonets and clubs?"

The red-haired man shook his head. "I have already taken care of it, General. Trust me on that."

"Do you hear this, Keeper? The general said, sounding rather aggravated. "The Colonel has taken care of it." He turned to the red-haired man, his dark eyes angry. "Please, Rogers. Enlighten me."

Ignoring the General's grouchy prodding, red-haired Colonel Rogers simply turned his attention back to the map. "I've simply devised another supply route. It's more perilous, but . . . it is one that those Yanks will never suspect." He reached into the pocket of his dress pants and retrieved a folded piece of yellowed parchment that he handed to the General.

"I took the liberty of simplifying things for you, sir," Rogers said. "This is a list of our regiment location coordinates and the dates that the supply caravan is expected to reach them. I've also included the estimated date for our final offensive."

The General scratched his beard, taking a long moment to glare at the page in front of him before Rogers tapped on the desk map once more. "See, sir . . . the new route will cut through here: up and over this mountain, instead of wasting the time to go around. Supplies of all kinds will reach every division in our Army . . . here . . . *here* . . . and here . . . and the Union forces will have no idea it's even happened."

"Come, now! This is impossible!" the General barked, clenching his wizened fist on the desktop. "We cannot take wagons over a mountain. Supply wagons would never be able to take this trail, Colonel!"

"General Lee, we don't use wagons," Rogers replied. "We use men and horses, a legion of them, all loaded with goods and ammunition. It's really quite something to see, sir."

General Lee pursed his lips and sighed. "It would have to be," he said, his voice much calmer. "And you believe it will work?"

Rogers let out a quiet laugh. "General, it's already working. The caravans set out nearly a week ago and they're making tremendous progress. Another week . . . ten days to be sure . . . and the divisions will be fully stocked. With this new route, what used to take a month's time will now take only half that."

With a slow nod, General Lee pushed his chair back from the desk and stood up, pulling an aged hat from his lap and fitting it onto his white-haired head. "Good," he said, slowly ambling around the desk, where Captain Keeper was now asleep, and stopping in front of the arched window. "Good work, Colonel. When the men have full bellies and full rifles, we will unleash an attack that will go down as one of the Confederacy's most devastating victories."

"This will be the battle that turns the tides," Rogers agreed. "And generations in the country's future will remember it as such."

Felicia knew it was time to go. She had no idea what these soldiers were talking about, but she was certain that they wouldn't want her listening in. Aside from that, her hunger reminded her that she hadn't yet achieved what she'd come here to do. Holding her breath, she ducked past the door, pausing a moment to make sure they hadn't noticed. Thankfully, with one of them asleep and the other two staring out the window, she may as well have been a phantom to them. Letting out her breath, she continued down the long hallway, pretending to dust the fixtures for several more paces until she came to a wide door on the left. Right away, it was clear that this door led into a large kitchen. Tucking her rag behind a large, painted portrait that hung on the wall, Felicia waited for a single soldier to pass by before she slipped into the kitchen.

The smell was enough to make her dizzy. What delicacies were being prepared in here? Meats and breads and fruits and biscuits . . . she had to keep herself from drooling. She cast a look around the room. In front of her, three women were manning an enormous stovetop and griddle, dishing out pancakes, fried eggs and thick slices of ham onto large serving trays. To the left, another woman was up to her elbows in soapsuds, scrubbing hard at a series of pots and pans to clean them. None of them knew Felicia was there at all. On her right side, the countertop held two towering plates of blueberry muffins and juicy sausage patties. Felicia set upon them immediately, stuffing as many of both items as she could into the pockets of her apron. The muffins were warm and toasty, and the sausages were still hot enough to cause a bit of pain on her bare hands, but she didn't stop. Only when she heard the sound of someone clearing their throat behind her did she halt her raid on the food plates.

Unable to mask the fear in her eyes, Felicia turned slowly to face the person who had caught her red-handed. With a muffin still in her hand, she raised her eyes, only to see the same young woman whom she had spotted out checking the laundry earlier. The woman, hands on her hips, looked Felicia up and down, her eyebrows furrowed in confusion. It was obvious she was putting the pieces together: a girl she didn't know, wearing a familiar apron, pilfering food while no one watched . . . it was obvious. It only took the woman a few seconds to realize that Felicia did not belong there.

Felicia tried to speak, but her nerves got the best of her, trapping her words inside her throat. Her eyes darted toward the door she had entered. If she ran, perhaps she could make it out and back into the woods before anyone started chasing her.

itchie Allen Greer

Unfortunately, her feet were rooted to the floor of the kitchen. She was practically paralyzed. The only thing she could do was feel her face and ears grow hot.

Strangely, the young woman didn't shout or call for help. She didn't attack or try to restrain Felicia. Despite clearly knowing what was happening in front of her, she simply gave Felicia a warm smile and turned back around to the soapy sink, plunging her hands into the steaming water.

Felicia let out a slow breath that she hadn't even realized she'd been holding. She didn't need any other hints. The woman was graciously letting her go, and go is what she was going to do. Sticking her head out of the kitchen, she found the long hallway to be empty and immediately started heading back in the direction she'd come from. Just when she thought she'd be able to make a clean getaway, voices issued loudly from the dining area. Heavy boot steps were coming toward the hall. Panicking, Felicia stepped to the left and ducked into the first room that she could, hiding behind the door just to ensure she wouldn't be seen. As the two men traipsed past her room, she breathed another sigh of relief, only to have it catch suddenly in her mouth.

She was standing in the exact study that General Lee and Colonel Rogers had been plotting in.

Fortunately, neither of those men was currently in the room. Through the arched window, she could see them standing outside, their heads bent together in some sort of important conversation. The only man still in the study was the rotund Captain Keeper, still snoozing on the front of the desk. He wasn't the only thing that caught her attention, though. On top of the desk itself was the unfolded piece of yellow parchment that Rogers had presented to the General, the one that Rogers had made up especially for him.

Felicia's mind was suddenly buzzing with thoughts. She wasn't sure exactly what the parchment was, but if she took it, maybe the grey coats wouldn't be able to launch their big attack that they were planning. That there was reason enough to pocket it.

As silently as she could with an apron full of sausage and muffins, Felicia tiptoed over to the side of the desk and leaned over it, her fingers outstretched. She was dangerously close to Captain Keeper. If she bumped into him, she was finished. She stretched further over the desk. She almost had it, almost had a grip on the parchment when a thick, meaty hand suddenly clamped around her wrist, making her gasp loudly with shock.

"I'm smellin 'me some blueberry muffins," said Captain Keeper, his bloodshot eyes blinking slowly at Felicia. His great, bristly mustache ruffled as he cleared his throat. "Ain't I?"

"Y—yes, sir," Felicia stammered, pulling a large muffin from her apron. "I . . . thought I would bring you some."

With her left hand, she handed him the warm pastry. While his drowsy eyes were fixed on it, she closed her right hand around the parchment and furtively slipped it underneath the apron and into the pocket of her trousers.

Keeper shoved the muffin into his mouth and closed his eyes again. "Mmm . . . you'd best . . . get a move on," he said, his lips smacking loudly as he chewed. "You ain't supposed to be in here."

Felicia nodded, trying to keep her adrenaline from making her lose control. "Yes, sir. Sorry, sir."

With his appetite sated, Keeper let his head fall back onto his fist, apparently determined to get more sleep. Felicia swallowed hard and backed out of the room, not even bothering to see if it was empty. Before anyone else could get more than a second's look at her, she hustled out the back door and made for the hill where Samuel and Isaac waited for her. She had something besides food, though; something that was sure to bring a right mess down on their heads.

***   ***   ***

Samuel nudged me with his elbow and pointed to the back of the big white house. I squinted my blurry eyes down at it and was able to see Felicia dashing out the back door and hurrying up the hill toward us. As she approached, Samuel and I slipped back into the cover of the forest and waited for her. After a moment, she crested the hill and crouched down low, scanning the tree line for us.

"Pssst!" Samuel called. "Over here!"

Following the sound of his voice, she scuttled over to where we were and dropped to the ground, lying back on the leaves as she panted for breath. "That was close," she breathed, wiping sweat from her forehead.

"Whatcha got?" Samuel asked, not even bothering to ask what she meant. "It smells good, whatever it is."

Sitting up, Felicia untied the apron from around her waist and pulled it off over her head before handing it to us. "Here," she said. "Save some for me."

Samuel and I wasted no time delving into the apron's pockets. I couldn't believe what she had managed to find. Never in our lives had we had such an incredible breakfast. The blueberry muffins were sweet and warm, soft and delicious. The sausages were simply amazing. They were juicy and still covered in grease . . . and I had never eaten anything better. As Samuel and I gorged ourselves, Felicia propped herself up on one elbow and reached into her pocket with her free hand, pulling out a partially wadded piece of yellowed parchment paper. Swallowing a huge mouthful of muffin, I took a drink of water from my canteen and nodded toward the paper.

"What's that?" I asked, taking another bite of my pastry.

Felicia sat up and flattened the paper out. "I ain't really sure. I took it from a couple of soldier guys. They made it out like it was real important."

"Why oo ake it?" Samuel asked his cheeks fat with food.

Felicia grabbed the apron away from us and grabbed one of the few remaining muffins. "I told you," she said, taking a small bite. "It was important to 'em. They're soldiers for the South, and the South is why we're slaves." She paused a moment, staring down at the treat in her hand. "Anything to mess them up . . . seems like a good idea to me."

Samuel leaned over and glared at the paper. "Hmm. Looks like a bunch of numbers. I know that much, at least."

"I can't read it, either," Felicia said, her face wrinkling in frustration.

I hesitated as I ate my final sausage. I had been keeping a secret from my brother and sister for a few months. I wanted to help them decipher the paper, but I wasn't sure how mad they'd be that I had kept such a thing from them. Ultimately, I decided it was an important enough occasion to come clean.

"Here," I said, wiping my fingers on the knee of my trousers. "Let me see."

Shrugging, Felicia handed the parchment to me. "Good Luck!"

I held the paper close to my face, blinking my eyeballs repeatedly to try and focus them. Having fuzzy vision was something I never could get used to. I suddenly missed Georgeo, the way he would encourage me when I was reading, the way he would spur me onward and help me only when I truly needed help. I definitely missed his spectacles. I hadn't given it much thought up till now, but I knew that I would likely never see him again. My best friend in the entire world . . . gone forever . . . without even a proper goodbye. The thought threatened to overwhelm me, so I did what I could to push it aside, focusing on the page in front of me instead.

Several of the words were still unfamiliar to me, but from what I could decipher, the parchment held the names of commanding officers for the Confederacy, as well as names of towns, dates, and several series of digits. I recognized the symbol of the small raised zero at the end of many of these numbers. It was meant to represent degrees. I had come across it once while reading and had asked Georgeo about it. He explained that it was used to represent either temperature or varying locations on a map. Judging by the sets of numbers on this page, I knew these were the map kind.

"Do you know what this is?" I asked Felicia, my heart rate beginning to rise.

She shook her head at me, her eyes wide in bewilderment.

"I think it's map locations," I told her, my voice hard as stone. "This part here says 'supply caravans' and it gives the dates that it's gonna be at these places."

Samuel squinted at me. "Since when do you read?"

"Caravans," Felicia said, leaning forward. "Yeah, them soldier fellas I took it from were saying something about supplies going over a mountain and a caravan reaching all their . . . divisions, or something."

"What's a supply caravan?" Samuel asked, looking as confused as ever.

"It's bullets and food and all that stuff," I said impatiently. "Stuff that soldiers need to fight battles. When they run out, supply caravans come to bring them more."

"I wonder if it's really important," Felicia mused, her eyes looking back toward the house she'd come from.

"This *is* important!" I said loudly. "This is *it*!"

"What do you mean?" she asked, her excitement beginning to match my own.

I shook the paper in my hand. "This has map locations of all the Confederate soldiers *and* the dates that they'll be ready to fight! And down here," I said, pointing at the bottom of the page. "It says 'final offensive' . . . and it gives a date."

"Final offensive?" Samuel echoed. "Like an attack?"

"What date?" Felicia asked.

I looked at the numbers on the page, trying to do some simple math in my head, which had never been easy for me, especially considering I'd never had any formal education on such things. "If I got my days right, it's less than two weeks away," I said gravely.

At once, Samuel was on his feet, pulling at Felicia's arm to help her up. "Come on," he ordered. "Get up. We gotta go."

Together, Felicia and I rose to our feet and began gathering our packs. "What are you doing?" I asked.

"You a dummy?" Samuel asked, staring over at me. "If they haven't by now, them soldiers is gonna realize soon that their plans are gone. And if it's as important as you're talkin' about, that's somethin' that would set the whole Confederate Army after us. So, come on. We gotta get outta here!"

"He's right," Felicia said. "By tonight, they'll have troops looking to hunt us down." She took the paper from me and stared down at it. "What have I done?"

"We gotta get that to the Union troops," Samuel said, shouldering his pack. "They can't be far. If we make it to that train in Chesterfield, I'm bettin' we find some blue coats soon after."

"Okay," Felicia said, folding the parchment carefully before slipping it back into her pocket. "Okay, let's go. Hurry. Back to the path and then we keep going North!"

Without any further discussion, the three of us fled into the forest, heading back towards the direction we had come from. We would have to be wary of slave hunters, but we were more worried about the squads of deadly rebel soldiers that would be sniffing at our heels before long. We ran fast and hard. Despite our painfully full bellies, despite how tired we were, our sudden fear was enough to propel us along. The thought of being captured by the enemy army itself was like a spur in our flanks, driving us through the forest. We'd been in trouble before, but this was a whole new level, something we had never experienced. Never before had so many dangerous people been angry with us.

For once, I was glad that Ma and Pa weren't here to see us.

*** *** ***

Back in the small study, sunlight poured through the arched window, falling across the shoulders of three men who were bent down. Captain Keeper, Colonel Rogers, and General Lee were scouring the desk and the surrounding floor area, sweat beading on their brows as they searched in vain. Maps were overturned, chairs were flung about the room, and the General's face was getting redder by the second.

"Come on!" Rogers said, wiping his forehead with the sleeve of his coat. "It has to be here. It can't have just up and vanished. It was here when the General and I stepped out. We were only gone for a few minutes, Keeper! You were still here. Did you see anyone else enter this room?"

Keeper righted an overturned chair and plopped his ample behind down into it. He was panting for air, practically exhausted after only a few minutes of physical activity. He dabbed at his thick mustache with a handkerchief. "No, there was no one!" he said. "Wait . . . actually . . . there was one slave girl. She came to bring me a blueberry muffin this morning. But she couldn't have taken—"

"You oaf!" Rogers bellowed, cutting across the Captain. "Of course she did! There's no other explanation!"

"Well, I—I didn't see anything!" Keeper stammered. "If she did take it, she's got to be around here somewhere."

"Search the house!" General Lee ordered. "Search the grounds, too. Round up every slave you can find and bring them inside for questioning. Do you think you can handle *that,* Captain?"

Keeper nodded his head and managed to get to his feet. "Yes, sir!" he barked. He stowed his handkerchief in his pocket and made to stomp out the door when Rogers' hand shot out to stop him.

"Captain," Rogers said. His voice was quiet, but oozing with venom. "If that paper gets into the wrong hands . . ."

"It won't, Colonel," Keeper said, his jowls wiggling under his chin as he spoke. "That won't happen."

Rogers nodded and removed his hand. "You'd better hope it doesn't."

Without another word, Keeper tottered out of the study, calling out for every soldier within earshot to drop what they were doing and assemble.

Removing his hat, Rogers scratched at his wavy red hair. "General, should I call off the attack, sir?"

General Lee leaned over the desk, resting his knuckles on the polished wooden surface. "No," he said after a moment. "No, we've put too much work into this. There is too much riding on this offensive, Colonel."

Rogers nodded. "I understand, sir."

"Do you?" Lee asked, standing straight as his eyes bored into Rogers'. "Because we are talking about a young girl, here, Nathaniel. One little slave girl who could spell disaster for the entire Confederacy! If she has associates, contacts, anything . . . if she left the grounds or passed that paper to someone else, it could be in Union hands by tonight!"

"I under*stand*, sir!" Rogers repeated. "Are you absolutely sure you don't want to call off the attack?"

Lee shook his head and took a few steps toward the window. "No, the attack will go ahead as planned. I'm trusting you to make sure that girl is found. It wouldn't hurt to send a small squad to track the surrounding areas."

Rogers nodded. "I'll tell Captain Keeper to put one together."

"Good," Lee said, crossing his hands behind his back as he stared out the window. "Because if we can't find her . . . if we all get trumped by one slave girl, well . . . then I don't believe we deserve to win this war. Do you?"

Rogers mashed his lips into a straight line. "I will make sure she is found, General. I vow to you."

Lee nodded. "You'd better."

Chapter 10

It was after dark before we stopped moving. Up till now, we had avoided traveling at night. With hazards like low visibility, nocturnal predators, and the simple eeriness of the woods after nightfall, it was much more dangerous than it was during the day. Tonight, though, it was necessary. We had to put as much ground as we could between us and the pursuers who were surely on our tails. Unlike the slave hunters, the men who were chasing us were trained and experienced killers. It was their business . . . and it was all the more reason to stay ahead of them.

We had finally exhausted ourselves well after the sun had gone down. Even the pinkish hue of twilight had faded into the night's greedy maw. We barely bothered with the bedding. We were too tired to care. Despite my sore body and my aching feet, it had still taken me a long while to fall into sleep. I don't know how long I had been out before the scurrying of a raccoon by my feet stirred me awake. I kicked at the creature to scare it away, making sure it had gone before I laid my head back down. To my left, Samuel was still sleeping and was snoring loudly in unison with the crickets. As I looked to my right, though, I saw that Felicia was still awake, her eyes staring up at the sky, searching the stars for the answers to whatever was on her mind.

I rolled over to face her and rested my head on my arm. "You need to rest," I muttered to her.

The sound of my voice gave her a small start, like she hadn't noticed me before I spoke to her. "I know, I . . . just can't," she said, returning her gaze to the stars. "What if I got something—right here in my pocket—that could make a difference in this war? What if this paper is something so big that it could end the fighting once and for all?"

She turned her head to look over at me, as if she were expecting me to give the answers to her question. "Well . . . what if?" I finally replied.

Once more she looked back to the sky. "We wouldn't be slaves no more, Isaac. None of us. We could be with Ma and Pa. We could be a family again."

"We *are* a family," I said to her. "You, me and Samuel . . . we're all each other's got. We gotta watch out for *us*."

"Don't you think I know that?" Felicia responded, turning her head toward me again. "And why are you talking like you just . . . forgot about Ma and Pa? Like they ain't part of our family no more?"

"I ain't talkin' like that!" I shot back, feeling the blood rush to my cheeks. "But you gotta use your head. Now that them grey coats know you got their plans, they're just gonna change 'em."

Felicia said nothing for a moment. Her hand slid down along her side until it came to rest on her pocket. "What if they don't?"

I sighed and blinked at her. "It's just a piece of paper," I whispered. I didn't know what kind of mad ideas were brewing in her head, but I had the feeling they weren't productive ones. She was daydreaming, seemed like, fantasizing about a world without the war, about having Ma and Pa back. She had been right. At that moment, I did feel like I had written them off, as if they were already dead. I hadn't intentionally thought that way, I just happened to realize it when she pointed it out. I still loved my mother and father dearly, but to keep from worrying all day about them, I had to push them from my mind. The guilt of this suddenly began to gnaw at me, and I felt tears filling the corners of my eyes.

"Maybe you're right," Felicia said quietly. "Maybe nothing'll come of it. But, I'll tell you what: them Rebs ain't gettin' me *or* this paper. No sir. I can promise you that!"

I sighed again and watched her stare up at the stars. Her determination was what kept us going. It's what had spurred us on through the wilderness for the past several days. But, at that moment, it was only frustrating to me. She was working herself up, hoping for a miracle. Young as I was, I still knew it was a bad idea.

"When we get on that train and head North, you can give it to the first Union man you see," I said to her, not wanting to argue anymore. "Then we can be done with it."

Felicia said nothing in response.

"You'd best get some sleep," I said, rolling onto my back. "You know you're gonna need it."

Without a comment, she simply turned over on her other side, facing away from me. Despite our briefly heated exchange, I still couldn't help but admire her. Her willpower was something I wished I possessed. I wished I had the fearlessness that she had grown into. As I looked over at her, I could almost see that she *had* grown in just a few days' time. I had begun to see it before, but now it was as plain as the nose on my face. She wasn't a little girl anymore, playing freeze tag and tripping on her own feet. She was like a strong young woman, ready to take on the world, or at least the entire Confederate Army. I guess having that piece of paper in her pocket gave her a mission. It gave her a purpose. I believe that's all anyone really wants in life: some meaning, their own purpose. No one really knows exactly what their purpose may be—big or small, early or late. That's not up to us to decide. It's up to the Creator. Even so, maybe she knew that night that her fate was tied to that paper. Maybe she could see something I couldn't. I guess it was possible.

As I lay there in the darkness, I couldn't help but wonder what my purpose was, though I hadn't been shown yet. I hadn't had the positivity that Felicia had acquired. I did have the sneaking suspicion that my time was coming. I didn't know what way or when, but I could feel it on the horizon.

All I could do was try to be ready for it when it hit me.

*** *** ***

As it turned out, Chesterfield hadn't been very far from where we had spent the night. When we arose the next morning, we packed up our belongings and only had to march a few miles under the morning sun before we had exited the forest and emerged onto the outskirts of the town. There had so far been no sign of slave hunters or soldiers as we crept through the city streets, but we weren't about to let our guard down.

As for the town itself, the sight of it was something that we weren't prepared for. The houses, most of them, were so tall and elegant, like Master Tomstin's. Not as big, for the most part, but just as splendid. They were built tall and narrow, and were painted with a great many colors, the likes of which, these eyes of mine had never before—such vibrant hues of red and yellow, such rich shades of blue and violet! There were shops and stores, some with young criers shouting loudly about the top quality wares that their particular employer was offering.

The streets weren't very crowded at such an early hour. It made sneaking through the outer blocks relatively easy. There were plenty of dark-skinned folk around the town, so we didn't look out of place, exactly. But we did make a point of following close behind some of the more affluent-looking citizens, just to give the appearance that we were traveling with them rather than on our own. It seemed to work because no one even gave us a second look.

As we arrived at the train station, our problem with blending in was less of an issue. People of both colors were bustling along the platforms, crowding each other and turning the station into a maelstrom of activity. As we ascended the small staircase to the platform, we melded seamlessly into the crowd, though our filthy, tattered clothing still made us easily identifiable. At the top of the stairs and to the left, a security booth was fitted between the two platforms. It must have been undergoing some repairs, because there were several boards and pieces of wood leaning against it. As the three of us crept along the side of it, we stepped around the boards and came upon a window into the booth. Curious, I chanced a look inside, only to let out a gasp that escaped before I could stop it. Instantly, I snapped my head away from the window and pressed my back up against the wall.

"What?" Samuel asked. "Who's in there?"

"Soldiers," I replied, keeping my voice as quiet as I could. Even with the noise of the commuters, I still didn't want to expose us. "There are soldiers talking to the station security guards."

"Look there," Felicia pointed past me and out onto the platform, where several more Confederate troops were worming their way through the crowd, searching every dark-skinned girl that they came across.

"They're everywhere," I said, feeling much of my hope drain away.

"Focus," Felicia said to me. "We need to find out where that train is going."

Samuel growled in exasperation. "Why do we need to do that? Seth told us it was going to Reading today."

"True, he did say it," Felicia agreed. "But I wanna be sure. I don't wanna get on the wrong train and go *back* South. Do you?"

Samuel sighed loudly, but didn't object any further.

"I bet just about every one of these people knows," Felicia said, her eyes scanning the area. "I bet they know when the trains are coming *and* where they're going. You two stay here out of sight. I'm gonna go ask and see if I can get some answers."

She pushed herself off of the wall and took a small step toward the platform, but Samuel reached out and grasped her arm, knocking loudly into some loose pieces of wood by his feet. Fortunately, no one seemed to notice, and he was able to stop Felicia before she left the shadow of the booth. "No!" He said urgently. "You crazy? They're lookin' for you!"

He pointed to the soldiers that were still searching the broadening crowd of civilians as they boarded the waiting train. They were paying close attention to the slave girls, ones that may have matched Felicia's description.

"You wait here," Samuel told her. "I'll go."

Felicia pursed her lips as she considered it, but she couldn't deny that his plan was a far less risky one. "All right," she relented finally. "But you be careful."

Without a moment wasted, Samuel was off. He made his way onto the main platform, staying relatively close to the security booth and trying to avoid rushing passengers and luggage carts.

"Excuse me, sir," he said, trying to catch the attention of a passing gentleman. Unsurprisingly, the man did not stop. He strode right by Samuel and didn't look back. "Pardon me, ma'am," Samuel tried again, this time attempting to appeal to a middle-aged white woman. She at least gave him a quick glance, but she did not stop either. Samuel made several more tries to get someone to speak to him, but it seemed that everyone was in such a hurry that they didn't take the time to answer. Finally, growing increasingly desperate, Samuel had no choice but to find a silver-haired man who was standing still and tug hard on the back of his white jacket. The man promptly turned around and looked down at Samuel, his eyes going wide.

"Mr. Kin?" we heard Samuel say in surprise.

"Samuel!" Kin exclaimed in shock, holding a pudgy hand over his heart.

At once, Samuel turned and fled, shoving his way past hurried passengers. He was trying his best to get back to us, but the crowded area was making it difficult for him to move. Mr. Kin, on the other hand, was someone that *other* people would move around, like river water around a large rock.

"Samuel, stop!" Kin called after him. "Stop at once!"

Before he could get back to us, Samuel slipped between two women in oversized dresses and was immediately scooped up into the thick arms of a tall, pale-skinned Confederate soldier.

"Whoa! Where you goin', boy?" the soldier asked, holding Samuel tight to his chest as he squirmed and kicked. "That's it, fight it. Go on. Gimme trouble and I get to lynch you from the first tree I find."

Felicia and I could do nothing but watch helplessly from where we stood behind the booth. Samuel was in the clutches of the enemy now. We could try to run out and save him, but it would only end up with both of us getting captured along with him. All we could do was watch as Kin waddled over to the soldier.

"This thing belong to you?" he asked, still struggling to hold onto Samuel.

"Yes," Kin said without missing a beat. "Yes, I always bring him with me on business endeavors. Cooking and cleaning, all of that, you know."

Felicia and I exchanged bewildered glances. What was Mr. Kin doing? Why was he lying to this soldier, claiming that Samuel belonged to him?

The soldier glared down at Samuel, who had gone still in his arms. "What you runnin' for, boy? You tryin' to escape? Huh?"

Samuel could only look up at the man, his dark eyes wide with fear.

The soldier looked back to Kin. "He run a lot?"

Mr. Kin nodded. "Well, yes . . . sometimes. I suspect he's got a bit of jackrabbit in him. Now, if you let him down, we'll be on our way, then."

The Confederate released his iron grip on Samuel, who dropped hard to the wooden platform before scrambling back up to his feet, taking a step toward Mr. Kin. "You know how to keep a jackrabbit from sprintin'?" the soldier asked, bending down to speak to Samuel. From the back of his leather belt, he produced a large, shining knife, the blade of which curved forward like a miniature wheat sickle. He tapped Samuel's thigh with the blade, making him jump.

"You cut that meaty part back there," the soldier said darkly. "Back of the leg. Then you're runnin' days would be over for sure. You don't want that, now, do ya?"

Samuel shook his head vigorously.

The solider smiled. "I didn't expect so. Now, I'm gonna let you go, but if I see you doing anything . . . *anything* . . . that I don't like, I will punish you accordingly—with your owner's permission, of course. You get me?"

Samuel nodded with verve.

"All right, then," the soldier said, standing straight. He gave a nod to Mr. Kin. "Carry on, sir." With that, he disappeared back into the crowd, searching for others to harass.

With the soldier gone, Samuel's face flooded with relief and he cast a glance over to where Felicia and I stood, our heads poking out from around the side of the booth. Unfortunately, Kin followed his gaze and looked over to us, his eyes meeting mine for a split second before Felicia and I retracted ourselves around the corner.

"Not good," I said. "Do we run?"

Felicia's eyes darted around the area, surely measuring the risk of being discovered if we were to start barreling through the crowd. Before she could give me an answer, though, Kin had reached us and was standing directly in front of us, his hand clasped tightly around the scruff of Samuel's neck.

"Let him go," Felicia said angrily, looking up at Kin past his protruding belly.

Kin held up his free hand in submission. "I intend to. In every sense of the word, young miss." He paused and craned his neck, looking over the horde of people. "You're the one they're after, aren't you?"

Felicia said nothing. Instead, she took a step backward and leaned once more against the security booth beside me. At that moment, I caught eyes with Samuel and was surprised to see that he seemed far less nervous than I was.

"Well," Said Kin, "it doesn't matter now. I want to help. I want to help Samuel, here." He patted Samuel on the shoulder. "He saved my life not one week ago. I wish to do the same for him."

"Oh, yeah? How you plannin' on doin' that?" Felicia asked harshly, having found her voice. She didn't even bother asking how Samuel had saved this man. I was glad of this. I would explain it to her later, if she wanted.

"I'm going to take him with me," Kin said, his face stony serious.

I pointed to the steel beast that waited on the track, spewing steam from beneath its metal hide. "You'll take him on the train?"

Kin nodded. "Yes, that's right."

"Where does the train go, exactly?" Felicia asked.

Kin lifted his plump hand and pointed down the track. "It goes North, my dear. Far away from all of this war foolishness."

Finally, Samuel felt the urge to speak up. "This is some kinda trick," he said skeptically, turning and facing Mr. Kin. "You gotta be lyin'."

Sighing, Kin hitched up his trousers and knelt down on one knee, something that seemed like a great effort for him. "Samuel," he said, looking directly at my brother. "That day back on Jefferson's plantation, you looked into my eyes then to see if I was lying to you. Do the same thing now, I implore you."

After chewing his lip for a moment, Samuel squared his shoulders and looked squarely into Kin's green eyes. The two of them simply stared at one another for a few seconds, Samuel searching intently for something that I will never comprehend. To his credit, Kin didn't move a muscle. He only waited for Samuel to render a judgment.

"He's tellin' the truth," Samuel finally said, his body relaxing a bit.

"You'll really take us with you, Mr. Kin?" I asked, unable to mask the hopefulness in my voice.

Kin looked at me gravely. "I am sorry, but . . . no. The offer is only for Samuel here. He is the one to whom I am indebted." The look on Kin's face, his wrinkled forehead, the remorse in his eyes, it made me believe he was genuinely sorry that he couldn't bring all of us. I was sorry, too. It would have solved our problem very nicely.

"Well, then you'll be ridin' alone," Samuel said matter-of-factly. "I ain't leavin' without my brother and sister."

Mr. Kin placed his hand on Samuel's shoulder. "The choice is yours, my boy. But, if you're thinking of taking that train . . . I would think again. It appears that a good portion of the Confederate Army is looking for you. There will be checkpoints along the way, at least until the track leaves the state. You'll be discovered before the day's end. If you decide to continue on foot, you'll likely last only another day or two . . . maybe a week, if you're good. There have been rumors of a Union regiment around this area, but that's still no guarantee of safety. If the rebels find you, they'll rectify whatever wrong you did by hanging you from the nearest tree. Shooting you, if you're lucky. At least allow me to save you from this terrible fate, Samuel. Your brother and sister would be glad to know you're safe."

To my left, Felicia slid down the wall. I guess Kin's words hit her harder than I had expected. To be honest, he had an irrefutable point. We hadn't anticipated the train stops being monitored. He was right. We would surely be caught and killed, even if we managed to get onto the train undetected.

"They *will* find you," Kin repeated. "Come with me, Samuel."

With his jaw set and his fists clenched, Samuel stood as straight as he could and shook his head. "I won't leave them. We've been though worse things than Confederates this past week. We will be fine on foot. So . . . you can just—"

The loud *clunk!* of a board across the back of his head cut him off in mid-sentence. Both Mr. Kin and I leapt back in shock, which was surprising considering how hefty Kin was. In front of us, Samuel's limp body crumpled beneath him and he sprawled face-first onto the platform. On the back of his shaved head, a lump was already visible. With my eyes wide with sudden fear, I spun my head to the left to see who had attacked him so harshly. Instead of a soldier or a slave hunter, I saw Felicia, tears in her eyes and a chunk of wood in her hand.

"What are you doing!?" I asked, not even trying to keep my voice down.

"I'm saving his life," Felicia answered, dropping the board. With a quiet sniff, she blinked away her tears and crouched down beside Samuel's unconscious body. "I'm sorry," she whispered, patting him on the head. "Goodbye."

"He will be grateful one day," Mr. Kin said, bending down to scoop my brother into his arms. "You two take care." As he turned to stroll back out onto the platform, Felicia tugged at his sleeve.

"Wait!" she said. As Kin turned toward her, she leaned down and kissed Samuel tenderly on the cheek. "I love you," she breathed into his ear.

As Kin turned once again, she let him leave, and I could only stare after him, hoping that Samuel had heard Felicia's parting words. A small part of me was still in disbelief that she felt the best option was to club him like an animal, but the rest of me knew that it was the only way to guarantee his safety. She had saved his life, just like she said. He wouldn't know it until he woke up, but it was true. I knew Samuel well enough to know that he would hate her for it at first. He would hate her for taking him out of the fight . . . because he knew we were stronger with him around. In time, though, he would become grateful. Kin was right about that. He would grow up free, he would have a family of his own, and he would know it was only because of the sacrifice that Felicia and I had made. We sent him to live, despite the fact that it meant we would surely die without him. I was glad she had done it, though. It was the right thing to do, even if it was difficult to watch.

I would mourn the departure of my brother later, but right now, there were other things to worry about. "Well," I said, watching Kin drag my brother onto the train with him. "What now? Should we run for it? Or should we try the train?"

Felicia let out a long, slow breath, her face hanging in melancholy. "I suppose we could take our chances on the train," she said. "If we can find a good place to hide, we can maybe make it across the state line."

I nodded. It wasn't a very sound plan, but we had limited options and none of them were very good. Aside from that, Samuel seemed to have taken much of our spirit with him when we sent him away. Perhaps it was just us doing everything we could to stay near him.

"I'm not sure how we're gonna get on board," Felicia said, scratching the braids on her head.

As I stepped up beside her, I noticed the other slaves carrying bags of luggage for their masters as they stepped onto the passenger cars. I also noticed that the soldiers who were guarding the doorways never paid much notice to those servant slaves, even the ones who were children. They were expecting the culprits to be traveling alone. As I scanned the mingling crowd, I spotted a very affluent husband and wife couple—or maybe husband and mistress, seeing as how young she looked—making their way to the departing train. The man wore a dark, pinstriped suit complete with top hat and cane, and the woman wore a very subtle navy blue dress, which looked like something Master Tomstin's own wife would wear. In one hand, the husband was attempting to carry his own sizeable leather suitcase, as well as his wife's powder blue bag, at the same time. They had no servant to help them, though, which gave me an idea.

"Come on!" I said to Felicia, pushing ahead into the crowd for the first time.

"What are you doing?" she asked from behind me.

I pointed to the husband and wife. "Just follow my lead."

Careful to stay low enough to avoid the gaze of the guards and soldiers, I sidled up next to the husband and placed my hand on the leather suitcase. He noticed at once, and looked down at me without stopping.

"Please, sir," I said with a tremendous smile. "Allow me to help you on board with your belongings."

The man slowed his pace, but now he and his wife were both staring down at me, their faces wrinkled in confusion. "Who the devil are you?" the man asked, keeping his grip on the bags.

I gave a gracious nod and continued smiling. "Compliments of the Chesterfield Train Station, sir. No need for payment."

The man's eyes flicked from me to Felicia, whose smile was mirroring the intensity of my own. Either he was in too much of a hurry, or he just plain didn't care, but he slowly released his grip on his bags, allowing me and Felicia to take the weight of them.

"Well, all right, then," he said flatly. "Come, come."

With both of his hands now free, the husband took the opportunity to puff out his chest and link arms with his beautiful companion. Making our way across the platform and onto the train, Felicia and I were careful to stay very close to the couple, often hiding behind the flaring ruffles of the woman's dress. As we stepped into the relatively dark, confined train car, we knew our plan had worked. We hadn't been spotted. We hadn't even been questioned. The chaotic activity outside was the perfect atmosphere to slip through the Confederates' tight grasp.

"Here we are," the husband said, turning back to us. With a grunt, he removed both bags from Felicia's hands and mine, placing them up onto the metal rack that ran a few feet above the seats.

"Well . . . carry on," the man said awkwardly, guiding his wife into the seat by the window.

Without knowing what to do next, Felicia and I turned and began strolling back up the aisle between the seats, wriggling past luggage-laden passengers who were still boarding. Without realizing it, we followed an elderly man through the door that connected the car to the next. When he sat down, I was able to finally get a good look at the train I was on.

It was no wonder the cars were so dark. The windows beside the seats were relatively large, but almost all of them had the shades drawn. I guess the passengers would rather forget about the madness just beyond outside. The seats were wide and covered in a bright red fabric. They were made to look like very springy benches, much more comfortable-looking than the ones on Tomstin's land. I suddenly had the urge to jump up and down on one of them. The floor and walls were paneled in rich, dark wood, though it was largely covered in a layer of dirt and dust, which took much away from the elegant appearance it was trying to achieve. On the ceiling, intermittent lanterns burned as brightly as they could, hung from fixtures that lined the center of the roof. They were just about the only things illuminating the space. The bad lighting would work in our favor, though, as Felicia pointed to a large storage trunk that was just to our right.

"There," she whispered. "Let's get in there."

As inconspicuously as possible, we shifted ourselves to the trunk and tried the lid, only to find it secured tightly. "No good," I whispered.

From the top of the trunk, Felicia pulled a thin red quilt, which had been embroidered with gold flowers, and used the cover of shuffling passengers to shove me down beside the trunk, pinning me between it and the back of the last seat in the car. Before I could even protest, she dropped down in front of me and threw the red blanket over both of us. Now, from the outside, our shapes would look like nothing more than an extension of the trunk. We waited on pins and needles for several long seconds, but it seemed that no one had noticed. Since I didn't want to risk speaking, I could only show my appreciation by squeezing her shoulder.

I don't know exactly how long we waited there, our breath turning the miniscule space into a blast furnace, but after some time, we heard a man making his way down the aisle of the train. His footsteps sent tremors through the wood flooring, making it feel like he was eight feet tall.

"Attention, ladies and gentlemen," the man said in a loud, clear voice. "My name is Captain Albert Sanford. There is no need to be alarmed at our presence. We are merely looking for three runaway slave children who may have stowed away. This is for your own protection, I assure you."

In front of me, Felicia's head tilted slightly at the soldier's words. Instantly, I knew she was wondering the same thing I was wondering: How did they know there were three of us? And then it dawned on me: there were eyes everywhere and someone must've spotted us as we were making a dash away from the house like three inexperienced burglars who had just committed their first crime.

Before I could think much more on the subject, Captain Sanford's voice rang out once more. "Sir, does this boy belong to you?" He asked.

"Oh, um . . . yes, of course, he does," a voice responded. My grip on Felicia's shoulder suddenly tightened. Underneath my fingers, I could feel her muscles tense. The Captain was talking to Mr. Kin.

"All right," Sanford replied. "If you would, please, show me his papers."

Mr. Kin scoffed. "I beg your pardon?"

"As I stated before," Sanford said sympathetically, "we are looking for three runaway slaves. Believe it or not, there have been traders and merchants who have assisted in the escape of owned slaves . . . using this very railroad, no less. If you'll just show me his documentation, I will be on my way."

"Oh, yes," Kin muttered anxiously. "Of course. I've got them somewhere."

Upon hearing an exaggerated rustling, I could only assume that Kin was making a show of going through his pockets. He was stalling for time, trying to think of some way to get Captain

Sanford away from him. All I could do was will him to succeed. Samuel's very life was riding on it.

"Must be here somewhere," Kin went on. "Where could I have put them?"

Sanford's patience had run out, though. "Sir, if you don't have the papers, this boy is going to have to come with me."

"He what?" Kin protested, trying his best to sound indignant.

"I think you both need to come with me, sir," Sanford continued. His tone had gone from polite to cold anger in just a few seconds. "Come with me . . . right now. I am going to order the conductor to remain in this station until my men have searched every inch of this train!"

A terrible iciness washed over me. We were going to be discovered. Samuel would be first, but the soldiers would scour the train until Felicia and I were found. All three of us would be dead by midday. The only chance we had was to wait until the soldiers were distracted with dragging Mr. Kin away. Maybe then, we could escape. The tables would be turned. It would suddenly be Samuel making the sacrifice so that Felicia and I could run away. I didn't care for the thought one bit.

As fate would have it, a third, unforeseen option was about to present itself.

As Kin and Sanford continued to argue, the trunk that Felicia and I were hiding next to began moving. It frightened me, at first, to see the lid of the trunk slowly lifting up, taking our blanket cover with it. I was sure that a soldier was discovering us. To the contrary, however, I saw the dark-skinned face of a man climbing *out* of the trunk. At a second glance, I saw that it was a familiar face.

"JoJo," I whispered. Apparently, he had listened to us about the train.

In an explosion of movement, JoJo threw open the trunk lid and leapt out into the aisle, tangling his feet in our blanket as he did. With a loud crash, he flopped hard onto the floor of the train before scrambling back to his feet and bolting out the door.

"You! Stop!" Sanford screamed, forgetting all about Samuel and Mr. Kin. "Men! Stop that slave!"

In a flash, Sanford had breezed right by us and out the door without even noticing we were there. We were uncovered and exposed, though, and the other passengers on the train were all too eager to point us out.

"There they are!" a man shouted.

"The kids are here!" a woman shrieked.

Felicia grasped my hand and shot upright, dragging me with her. "Come on!" she shouted, dragging me off the train. To our fortune, every guard and soldier on the platform had joined in the chase for JoJo, leaving me and Felicia undetected as we fled the platform and headed back into the town, searching for a place to hide. When we were about a hundred yards from the station, we stopped outside a beat-up saloon and ducked between several waiting horses. Hidden amongst the animals, we turned our attention back to the station, looking past it at the small shape of JoJo as he sprinted up a grassy hill in a desperate bid for freedom. He had a good lead on the men chasing him, but there were just so many of them, more than I would have imagined, and they weren't going to let him escape. As we watched, one of the Confederates let off a single shot from a pistol . . . and JoJo's body pitched forward onto the ground. He didn't move again.

"Oh!" Felicia gasped. "No!"

As the legion of troops closed in on their kill, the train finally let out a tremendous hiss and screech as a towering pillar of black smoke shot into the sky. Within a few short seconds, it was on its way, slowly picking up speed as it chugged North with Mr. Kin and Samuel both still on board.

"Goodbye, Samuel," I said, still catching my breath from our run.

Felicia nodded. "We still need to go North. We need to find the Union troops."

"Well, the train idea ain't gonna work," I said sarcastically, watching the black smoke get further and further into the distance. "What now?"

Felicia turned and looked up at the saddle of the horse she was standing next to. "We done it once already," she said, giving me a hint of a smile.

I turned to the horse that I was hiding behind and looked it over. None of them were laden with supplies like the last ones had been, but they would definitely do in a pinch. As I saw it, our situation would definitely qualify as a pinch.

With a nod of agreement, we placed our feet in the stirrups and hoisted ourselves onto the backs of two horses, both of which must have belonged to men in the saloon. With a tug on the reins, we were able to free them from the post they were lashed to.

"Let's find us some Yankees," Felicia said with a grin. Giving the horse a nudge, she turned and headed back toward the station with me on her heels.

To my surprise, Felicia didn't seem like she was trying to avoid the dozens of guards and soldiers on the hill. Her path looked like she planned on charging right past them. I didn't exactly find this to be the most intelligent plan, but I couldn't deny feeling a bit of excitement at the thought. The horses weren't used to us as riders, so we weren't able to do any fancy maneuvering, but we could make them run. That was all we needed.

As Felicia and I stormed past the train platform and left the edge of town, we powered straight ahead, straight for where JoJo lay motionless on the side of the hill. Upon seeing us approaching, several of the guards and soldiers stopped to stare incredulously at us, as if they couldn't believe what they were seeing. I wasn't complaining. The longer they stood there dumbfounded, the better our chances would be of getting away. I couldn't fight the smile from spreading wide across my face. As we began to pass the lot of them, however, my eyes suddenly fell upon something that made my grin vanish completely. I don't know how I saw him, standing there in the middle of several dozen Confederate soldiers, but I instantly understood how Captain Sanford had known there were three of us. I hadn't even considered the possibility, but, it was undeniable, staring me right in the eye as I rode past him.

Once again, appearing where I least expected him, was Mr. Cornelius Slate, not in a cotton field, not sleeping under a tree, but looking as angry as ever and working with Rebel soldiers to hunt us down. I barely had time to process what I had seen before the first gunshot rang out.

"Head down!" Felicia screamed back at me. "Yah! Yah!" She kicked her horse hard to coax more speed from it, cracking the reins against its back. I mimicked her movements, feeling slightly sorry for my horse even amidst the chaos.

I don't know how many shots popped off behind us—six or seven—but we managed to bypass JoJo's body and ride up and over the hill in a matter of seconds. Neither of us had been hit, thankfully. I was also glad that the rest of those men would have to run on foot back to town before they could get their wagons and horses in order. This delay would give me and Felicia a sizeable head start. As we descended the other side of the green hill, the train blew its loud whistle, roaring triumphantly as it steamed off into the distance.

"Go, Samuel! Go!" Felicia shouted merrily, whooping loudly into the air.

Behind her, though, I couldn't share her joy. I didn't know if she had seen what I had, but all I could feel was a familiar icy dread hanging over me. I felt like I had been caught stealing by a parent and was now dreading the punishment that was sure to follow. When we had left Slate out in the wilderness with no horses or shoes, it had been hilarious to me. I had relished that victory. Now that he had somehow found his way to us, I knew he would be furious, I knew he would be out for revenge, and all I could do was regret the fact that we had stolen from him. Perhaps it was because I had both seen and felt his particular brand of punishment, but I knew what Slate was capable of. I couldn't deny . . . I was afraid.

We rode North at a steady pace for nearly an hour, knowing full well that a squad of angry Confederates was surely not far behind us. My neck began to ache from constantly twisting to look over my shoulder. I almost felt like it would have better if I could see them. That way, I would at least know where they were. They could be flanking us on either side and we would never know. The rolling hills would offer me a brief moment of clarity as I reached the top and could see further around the landscape, then I would head down the other side, feeling more vulnerable as I got lower.

We passed through gorgeous fields of golden wheat, waving serenely at us in the wind. We rode through small streams and creeks, even patches of forest, but we couldn't stop to appreciate their beauty. We were pushing our horses too hard. We needed to stop. At the edge of a wild-looking tract of forest, we finally came to a stop, allowing the horses to catch their breath a bit.

"This is too thick for them," I said to Felicia. "We can't ride through here."

Felicia stared down at the mean brush and sighed. "Well, if it's too thick for our horses, it'll be too thick for *their* horses."

"What you wanna do?" I asked.

Felicia shrugged her shoulders. "We go on foot. We're gonna climb to the top of the next hill and see if we can see some blue coats."

I scratched my bushy hair nervously. "And if we don't?"

"No time for 'what ifs'," Felicia said, sliding off of her horse. "Come on. Get on down and take off that saddle."

There was no questioning her this time. As valuable as the horses were, we couldn't take them into the overgrown forest and we didn't have the time to look for an alternate route. As I began undoing the buckles, I gave the horse a pat on the shoulder. "Thanks, buddy," I told him. "You're free, now."

Both saddles dropped onto the ground, but the horses only strolled away at a leisurely pace. They were probably too tired from the ride thus far. They were likely going to try and hunt down something to drink. As for me and Felicia, we had other things to worry about.

"Oh, no," Felicia said, pointing over my shoulder. "There they are! Come on!"

As she lowered her head and plunged into the woods, I spun around to look behind me, staring in terror at the wave of Rebel troops galloping over the distant hills. I don't know how, but there seemed to be more of them than before, covering entire hillsides as they rode closer. I wasn't about to wait for them to arrive, though. Using my fear as fuel, I turned and barreled into the thick greenery.

I immediately felt the resistance. Tangled webs of brambles and vines had laced themselves together between the bushes and trees, acting like a never-ending series of nets that were strategically placed to trip you or direct you around a tree into a trap of prickly shrubs. My clothes were almost like shackles as I tried to make my way through. Sleeves and trouser cuffs were shredded and tattered as I struggled onward. The thorns dug into my flesh from every direction. I couldn't even begin to count the places from which I was bleeding. I was panting hard, sweating bullets, even under the shady canopy of the forest.

Finally, it seemed we were passing the worst of the mess. I felt the overwhelming urge to stop and rest until I heard the shouting from behind me.

"Fan out and move in!" Someone ordered.

"They're here!" I whispered to Felicia, who was several paces ahead of me. As I opened my mouth to call out again, though, my right foot stepped into a thick, moist carpet of moss and slipped right out from under me, throwing me down to the ground. At once, the sharp pain in my ankle was enough to make me cry out.

"Isaac!" Felicia blurted, hustling back to me. She grabbed my left arm and draped it over her neck as she stood up, pulling me off the ground as she did. "Come on," she said, gasping for breath. "Come on, we gotta keep going!"

We hobbled along as best we could for a few yards, all the while listening to the soldiers gaining ground behind us. The sounds of twigs and vines snapping were growing louder with each passing moment. It wouldn't be long until they were upon us. My ankle was still throbbing, but it wasn't as agonizing as it had been. I was able to walk more freely, but that didn't stop the soldiers from gaining on us. They sounded off to one another through the trees, making sure they stayed in a straight line. The sheer volume of overlapping voices was enough to grip me in a state of severe trepidation.

We were approaching the edge of the tree line. Beyond the thick woods, I could see the hill sloping down into a hollow before rising back up to another ridge that was eighty or ninety yards away. I almost didn't want to leave the forest. Without it, we would be exposed and very vulnerable. We'd be sitting ducks.

It seemed Felicia was thinking the same thing I was. We couldn't have been more than a minute ahead of the troops when she stopped us next to a large, ivy-covered tree a few feet from the tree line. "Down there," she pointed, too out of breath to elaborate. Before I could ask what she meant, she had shoved me down to the forest floor where I landed on the thick growth of ivy. Quickly, she dug underneath the carpet of slender green vines and lifted them up, creating a small space that we both wriggled into. With some adjustment, we arranged the ivy over ourselves and lay as still as we could, catching our breath as the soldiers closed in.

In a matter of moments, they were there, shoving their way through the thick growth, slicing at brambles and branches with cavalry swords and bayonets. Felicia and I kept quiet, peeking through the ivy as they continued to call out to each other. Heavy black boots were just inches from where we lay, treading on the vines that concealed us. I slowly adjusted my head so that I could sneak a look at the man above me. Unfortunately, all I could see was a long, narrow nose and some red hair poking out from his hat.

"Careful, boys," he called out. "See that flag over there? Yanks are right over there on that next hill. We aren't looking to start a firefight if we don't need to, so stay in the trees."

"Yes, sir, Colonel Rogers," the nearest soldier replied. The message was relayed again and again through the line of troops until all of them knew of the Union's position. I couldn't help but feel overwhelmingly frustrated. The blue coats were just on the next hill! If I hadn't fallen and twisted my ankle, we might have been able to make it there. We would have been safe. They would have taken us in, listened to our story, and Felicia could have given them her Rebel information page. Our journey would have been over.

Now, we were stuck beneath an ivy plant, feeling the worms and beetles crawling underneath our bodies, watching a squad of men hunting us with the intent to kill. We couldn't be much worse off than we were. As Colonel Rogers stepped away from us to search somewhere else, Felicia began to stir next to me, her breath speeding up again. Very slowly, she twisted her head over to look at me.

"No matter what," she breathed. "You stay here."

My eyebrows instinctively pulled together in confusion. What in the world was she planning now?

"I'm going for the Union," Felicia whispered. "I can make it."

I shook my head slowly. "No you can't. You won't make it."

"I have to," she replied.

She took my hand in hers and squeezed it tightly, making sure I squeezed back. Even in the darkness, I could see the tears forming in her eyes. Just the sight of them made my own eyeballs well up.

"Stay here," she whispered again.

I didn't have the time to argue any further. In a flash, she had released my hand and shot up to her feet. After taking a moment to fix the ivy over me, she gave me one last wink and took off at a run, clearing several steps before anyone even noticed her.

"There she is!" Someone finally shouted.

"I see her!"

"Stop her!"

Footsteps were suddenly coming from all directions, thundering around my hidden body as they converged on the tree line just beside me. It was all I could do to keep from getting up and running after Felicia. I didn't like being stuck here with all these dangerous men. I didn't like it one bit. My arms and legs were tensed like a coiled snake. I was ready to flee at a moment's notice.

Suddenly, I could hear Felicia's voice. It was faint, but she was definitely calling out, presumably to get the attention of the blue coats. I didn't know what I was expecting, perhaps a reply from the Union leader, but I was silently hoping and praying that they would be able to hear her in time. Her life depended on it.

"She's headed for the Yankee camp!" One of the soldiers shouted.

"Stop her!" screamed Colonel Rogers. "She's carrying sensitive information! Stop her at all costs! Open fire!"

I think my heart stopped at those words.

The air was suddenly vibrating with what seemed like a million gunshots. I slapped my hands over my ears, letting the echoes of the shots drown out my scream. Immediately, gun smoke had filled the trees, and was coalescing together in a stinking fog that threatened to choke me. It was the last straw for me. I had to get up. All the Rebels in front of me had fired their weapons, and I needed to see if Felicia was all right.

With lightning speed, I thrashed my way free of my ivy blanket and stood, almost oblivious to the threat around me. Though, with the smoke still lingering—and with their focus primarily on Felicia—no one seemed to even notice me. I was able to watch as Felicia continued running toward the next hill. I could still hear her shouting, and it seemed that the Union troops had heard her, as well. If they hadn't, the gunfire surely had their attention. A squad of blue coat soldiers was carefully stepping into view, their guns trained on the forest.

"Shoot her!" Colonel Rogers bellowed again. "Don't let her get away!"

By now, several of the Confederates had reloaded their rifles, and more gunshots rang out. I didn't cover my ears this time. I didn't do anything. All I could do was watch the small figure that was Felicia dashing toward freedom while balls of lead exploded into the dirt around her.

"Go," I said quietly, watching her run. "Run faster!"

Growling with frustration, Colonel Rogers turned to his right. "Wilson!" he shouted. Next to him, the thin, pale-skinned man named Wilson dropped to one knee.

"I got 'er," Wilson said, tilting his head to stare down the long barrel of his rifle. My stomach suddenly did a backflip in my gut. This man wasn't like the others. The way his smooth brow wrinkled with focus, the way his green eyes narrowed into the distance . . . I knew he wasn't going to miss. Before I could say or do anything to stop him, he squeezed the trigger.

I watched the recoil of the rifle jar his shoulder, but then I turned my attention back to Felicia, just in time to see her body stiffen in shock before dropping to the grass. She had been hit square in the back.

Chapter 11

"NO!" I roared.

I couldn't control it. At that moment, my sense of self-preservation had vanished. The only thing left was the unspeakable horror of witnessing my own sister get shot like an animal. My eyes and mouth were hanging wide open. This couldn't be real! That couldn't have *really* just happened . . . could it? Felicia was beginning to crawl, dragging herself toward the Union soldiers, who were massing on the hill. One of them began making his way down to her. I had to get there. I had to help her get to safety. I had to save her. I broke into a run, took two steps, and felt the butt of a rifle smash into the right side of my head.

My vision was instantly white, nothing but blinding, disorienting whiteness. There was a very high pitched ringing in both my ears, which distorted the noises of the world. Everything was muffled, as if I were under water. I landed hard on my left shoulder, my limp body practically splattering onto the forest floor. I don't remember falling, but the impact was enough to mostly clear my senses. My hand instinctively slapped over the spot where I had been struck, feeling the blood that was seeping out of my torn flesh. I could feel my pulse under the wound, which disturbed me. As I blinked repeatedly, doing my best to rid myself of the grogginess, a heavyset, bearded Confederate soldier emerged above me, smiling down at me as he cocked the hammer of his revolver.

"That's as far as you're goin', boy," he drawled.

At that moment, I heard a strange crackling sound in the air. At first, I believed it to be my ears still trying to recover from the blow to the head. As the bullets began whizzing above me, I knew that it was actually the sound of the Union returning fire.

With a loud, resounding *thud,* the heavyset soldier above me took a shot in the upper chest, which sent him toppling backwards with a strangled cry of pain and surprise. Around me, several more men let out shrieks and grunts as they felt the sting of the blue coat volley. This was my chance. While the Rebels were taking cover, I could escape and make my way to Felicia. She still needed my help. I could get to her now. As I made to get up, though, a powerful boot planted itself in my ribcage and forced me back down to the ground. Looking up, I saw that the boot—or rather, the foot inside the boot—belonged to none other than Cornelius Slate, looking more menacing than I had ever seen him. Like the last man, Slate held a revolver in his hand, with six shots that he would never miss with.

My fear and frustration were boiling over, now, and I did the only thing I could think of. I begged.

"Mr. Slate, please!" I shouted, trying to be heard over the sound of the Confederate guns. "You have to let me go!"

I stared up into the tinted lenses that concealed his eyes, waiting for a response. There was none.

"Please, Mr. Slate!" I went on, feeling tears dripping out of the corners of my eyes and into my shaggy hair. "Please, you have to let me help her! They're gonna kill her!"

Slowly, Slate turned his head to stare out at the hillside. He didn't even flinch as more Union bullets zipped through the leaves around him. The Rebels were still firing, as well. Though, I wasn't sure they were trying to hit the Yankees or Felicia.

"She's the only family I got left, Mr. Slate," I sobbed, my voice breaking badly. "I don't want her to die!"

Slate turned his attention back to me, the dark lenses masking whatever thoughts his eyes may have otherwise betrayed. I couldn't tell what was on his mind. I couldn't tell what he was going to do. I waited for several seconds before he reacted at all. His frown, ever present on his lips, relaxed into a straight line as he lifted his boot off my chest.

I looked up at him, blinking the wetness from my eyes and wiping my nose with the back of my hand. I could hardly believe it, but he was letting me up. I wasted no time in scrambling to my feet and fleeing the tree line, shoving my way past several soldiers as I went. Bursting out of the tree line, I searched for Felicia and found her, still crawling, reaching out to a Union solider who was lying next to her.

"There goes another one!" I heard Colonel Rogers shout from behind me. "Wilson! Take him down!"

Oh, no. Not Wilson. He wouldn't miss in a hundred years, not from so close, anyway. I tried to juke to the left, hoping to throw off his aim. If I could survive the first shot, I could be much further away before he was able to reload and try again. As I ran, though, four successive shots resonated from behind me. Not slowing down, I turned my head around to see Slate, standing with his revolver still smoking, watching as two bodies slumped to the ground. To my surprise, Cornelius Slate had shot Wilson and Colonel Rogers dead. Of all the people in the world, he would be the last that I would expect to lift a finger to help me, much less do anything of this caliber.

As I began to look away, I was able to catch a glimpse of two other Confederates charging at Slate. To this day, I still don't know for sure, but I thought I saw Cornelius Slate smile as the two Rebels drove their bayonet blades into him and tackled him to the ground. He didn't even try to fight them.

As terrible as it was to see, I couldn't stop. I couldn't take the time to mourn for Mr. Slate, even though it was apparent that—for whatever reason—he had given his life for me. I poured on every bit of speed that my legs could muster as I flew down the hill, feeling the earth tremble with each bullet that slammed into the grass near me. Felicia was growing larger. I was drawing nearer, near enough to see the blood that had soaked her clothes. Beside her, a Union soldier clutched her hand, which contained the parchment of Rebel supply routes. I couldn't tell for certain, but it looked like she was whispering something to him. As I began to run up the hill to them, a small handful of blue coat troops reached them first—two of them firing towards the Confederates as the rest dragged Felicia and the wounded man to safety.

"Wait!" I called after them. "Felicia!"

They didn't wait, however, and I was glad. They were able to carry Felicia and the soldier to the top of the hill where they were concealed by forest. I was at least glad that she was out of danger. Unfortunately, that left me alone in the open, the sole remaining target for the Confederates. If there was ever a time that I needed my speed, it was now.

I can't tell you how many bullets were hissing through the air, like angry insects whizzing by my ears. The popping of the guns behind me was sparse and random, like corn in the kettle. I don't know how, but I was able to avoid every one of them. As many shots as were fired at me, not one hit me. Even the Union troops seemed surprised to see me as I made it to the top of the hill and dashed to where Felicia and the injured man lay on the grass. Beside her, a healthy Union solider was guarding both of them while another one was looking over her wounds. He must have been a doctor.

"Nothing I can do, sir," the medic said to the wounded Yankee.

"Rally the men," wheezed the bleeding solider, who was clearly the Captain of the squad. "Charge those Rebs and push them back."

The medic nodded. "Yes, sir."

As the medic sprinted away to gather more troops, I dropped to my knees and skidded on the grass to where Felicia rested. I could barely see from the tears that were welling up in my eyes. There was so much blood on her clothes, on her skin. I didn't know a person could hold that much of it in their body. I clutched her free hand, but her attention was on the Union Captain, who had crawled over and tilted his ear to Felicia's blood-stained lips.

"Did . . . you look?" she gasped. "Did you . . . see?"

The Captain nodded, handing the paper to the soldier that was guarding all of us. "Yes," he breathed. "Enemy locations. I see it. Thank you, young lady."

"Sir," said the guard. "How can we know this information is trustworthy?"

The Captain looked over at him and coughed before answering. "Lieutenant, this girl has an entire garrison pursuing her. They clearly thought this information was important enough to merit such an attack. That tells me it is genuine. Doesn't it you?"

The Lieutenant nodded and closed the parchment in his bony fist. "Yes, sir."

With a trembling hand, Felicia reached out to the Captain, pulling him back toward her. I leaned forward, too, eager to hear anything she had to say.

"Win . . . this . . . war," she choked out. "Free . . . my people."

The Captain nodded again, a single tear rolling down his cheek. At that moment, the medic came sprinting back through the forest, dropping down next to the Captain with a leather bag in his hand. "Hold on, sir!" he shouted. "I need to get these bullets out. Captain, the men are waiting for you to lead the charge."

At once, the guard rose to his feet and bolted through the trees. "On me, men! On me!" He screamed at them. "CHARGE!"

The forest erupted with the adrenaline-fueled shouts of the Yankee troops as they barreled out of their cover and charged full tilt toward the Confederates' position. The Rebels fired off several more shots as the blue coats flooded toward them. Several of the Union men dropped to the ground, but the rest continued on, surging toward the enemy with burning fury on their breath.

I turned my attention away from them and back down to my sister, who was on her back, staring up at the clear, blue sky. Her eyes, blinking slowly, shifted over to meet mine. I smiled, unable to stop the tears from spilling over my lashes.

She gave me a weak smile in return. "Isaac," she breathed. "We . . . did it."

I clutched her hand tightly in both of mine and shook my head, drawing in a shaky breath.

"No. No, *you* did it. It was you. You saved me. You saved us all."

"You . . . saved me, too," she said, smiling before launching into a coughing fit that sprayed flecks of blood all over my lap. "Tell Ma . . . and Pa . . . I love 'em."

Her words were like knives in my heart. I hugged her limp hand to my chest and squeezed my eyes shut, forcing more tears out of them. My anguish, though overwhelming, emerged as only a whimper from my lips.

"Will you . . . tell them?" Felicia asked, her voice pleading.

Unable to form any coherent words, I nodded my head. Behind me, maybe a billion miles away, the sounds of battle echoed on the warm summer air. Shouting, gunfire, metal clanging against metal, it was all just faint noise, like it wasn't even real.

"Hey," she rattled, trying to control the convulsions that were taking over her body. I opened my eyes and looked down at her, letting a loud sob tear its way out of my throat.

Slowly, and with great effort, she lifted her hand from my chest and rested it against my dirt-smeared cheek. "You're it," she said.

From somewhere in the back of my mind, I heard my father's words reaching out from my murky depths of my memory. "*Sometimes, a touch of a hand is all a person needs."* Pa's voice echoed. *"Lots of comfort to be had, just in the touch of someone who cares. It's how we know we ain't alone in the world. It's how we know . . . even in the most troubling of times . . . that everything's gonna be okay."*

A small grin broke across my face as I looked down at my dying sister, though it immediately began to fade. Her hand slipped from my cheek, but I caught it before it could fall to the ground. Felicia's eyes were suddenly glassy, her body was still. Her hand was now lifeless in mine, stained red and growing colder by the moment.

I tilted my head forward and rested it against her ribcage, letting my sorrow escape my lips in a series of raw, ragged howls. I don't know how long I sat like that, my body draped across her torso, before I felt hands pulling me gently away from her. Through my puffy eyes, I saw men in blue uniforms around me. The Union. They were collecting Felicia and the injured Captain, who was still being tended to by the medic. I knew I was in good hands, so I let myself go. I gave in to my exhaustion and let my eyes close as they carried me away. I didn't even care where they were taking me.

That was the last moment I spent with my sister.

Epilogue

Any amateur history buff will tell you that the Civil War officially ended on April 9, 1865. Technically, just about anyone would say they're right. As for me, I personally believe the war ended that day, on top of that grassy hill in the middle of nowhere, when Felicia handed that paper to the Union. The Northern forces were able to use the information on it. They were able to find the Confederate supply route, and they were able to stop the offensive that General Lee had in the works. The entire course of the war, the course of the Nation itself, was changed that day. All because of what Felicia had the courage to do. I often think how amazing it is, how mind-boggling, that all that change could come from one single piece of paper. Such a small thing. It still overwhelms my mind to this day.

Every day, I wish that Felicia had survived with me. I wish I could have celebrated with her. I wish I could have stood beside her as we greeted our mother and father as a family, finally free from the bonds of slavery. Regrettably, I could not. She had fulfilled the purpose that she had been given. Her destiny led her up on that grassy hill that day. I don't think she had a choice. Though, if she had, I know she'd have done the exact same thing. She had embraced her purpose. I know now . . . that's what I was there for. The threads of my destiny were tied to hers.

I have often thought it was a miracle that I survived that battle. Not only did I survive, I had escaped virtually any kind of injury. It had to have been the grace of the Creator that shone down upon me, guiding my steps, making sure that every single bullet fired at me never found its mark. Whereas Felicia had been meant to give her life that day, I was meant to live on. Her story was fated to end there, and my purpose . . . was to tell it.

It's been twenty-five years, now, since Felicia drew her last breath. Twenty-five years since I felt her touch or heard her voice. On the hill where it happened, there is a life-sized stone statue of her that stands, not just as a marker for her body, but as a reminder of what she accomplished.

I remember the first time I looked up at the shining, marble statue of my sister. It had taken a quarter of a century, but finally, her contribution to the Union troops had been recognized. Because of the story I wrote, the story detailing the journey of three runaway slaves, the state had agreed that Felicia deserved to be honored. The statue, which depicted her in mid-stride, running fast with a piece of paper held in her hand, sat just outside of Chesterfield, which had grown considerably since I last saw it. With my descriptions, the artist had recreated her image with startling accuracy. Just looking up at her face again brought back all sorts of memories. I left a copy of my book, *Running South*, there at the feet of the statue, just in case anyone wished to read the story that she belonged to.

On the day that the statue was erected, my entire family had turned out, as well as a handful of others, to pay tribute to the girl who helped end a terrible war and free thousands of slaves from their chains. My father had beamed proudly at the statue, his kind eyes filled with joy at seeing his only daughter immortalized in such a way. My mother had been with him, weeping silently, but also proud of the things her baby girl had done for us all. It had been good to see them all again, especially Samuel, who had moved back South after the long war had ended.

Mr. Kin had taken excellent care of Samuel, beginning on that day when the train had carried them both North. Ever grateful for the time that Samuel had saved his life, Mr. Kin had left a large sum of money to Samuel when he'd died, and my brother had used it to build a police station in his new home town, which had been sorely needed. In doing so, he became the first African-American police officer that any Southern state had ever seen. I was proud of him for that. It was hard work, especially earning the respect of people who weren't used to seeing a black man in such a position. But, he fought through it. Because of that, he would have my respect forever.

Even my old friend, Georgeo Tomstin had turned up, which had surprised the daylights out of me. He was finally able to officially meet my family, as well as my beautiful wife, Helen, and my son . . . whom I had also named Georgeo, in honor of my childhood friend. We're still in touch now. After twenty-five years, we have a lot of catching up to do. He had a wife and child of his own, as well. I can't wait to meet them.

It was a good day. When my son had asked me who the statue was, I had told him it was his aunt, the bravest girl I had ever known. I remember that he'd asked me if she knew we were there, if she knew that all the people had gathered just to honor her.

"She knows," I had told him. "Your grandfather once told me that nothing is stronger than a family's bond, and he was right. Your Aunt

Felicia is gone, yes, but she's looking down and watching over us . . . just like I will one day be looking down to watch over you."

Such a thing was easy to explain to him. I think, deep down, he knew it was true. What wasn't so easy, however, was trying to explain why—even though we were free—there were still certain things that we still couldn't do, things like sitting in the same rows of theaters or drinking from the same water taps as white people. All I could do was convey to him that, although America was a great land, it still had much to learn, and such a thing would take time. For now, all we could do was be grateful for the liberties we did have.

Not one hour goes by that I am not grateful—to the men that fought the war, yes, but also to my beloved sister, whom I miss each day. Because of her, I have a wonderful wife and an incredible son. She sacrificed everything so that thousands of families just like mine could live without fear. Sometimes I still feel her, tapping me on the shoulder like we're playing freeze tag again, I still hear her whispering to me if I listen hard enough, and I still see her face in every young girl that I pass on the streets. To this day, I still speak to her, even if just to thank her for everything she did, and to let her know that, if I have anything to do about it, the whole world will one day know her story. I hope that everyone will eventually learn of that courageous little girl who found the strength and conviction to help end a war . . . and unite a nation.

The End

About The Author

As a young boy, Ritchie Allen Greer had dreamed of one day writing a great novel, which seemed out of reach, since at no time was he considered an intellectual type. But as he grew up, he quickly discovered that he had a passion for writing and creating great stories that not only captured people's minds but also grabbed their hearts.

Ritchie's dream of writing took him from his small town of North Wilkesboro, NC to Los Angeles, CA where he lives today with his girlfriend. He has two wonderful teenaged kids and hopes that through his passion and perseverance, he would be able to provide a better life for them as well as teach them to follow their dreams, no matter how beyond their reach it may seem.